DEADLY ABDUCTION

A CHRISTIAN ROMANTIC SUSPENSE

GRAYSON'S GUARDIANS
BOOK 1

LAURA SCOTT

1

———

Grady "Mac" McFarland stared at his boss, Rex Grayson. Normally, he gave his former army captain a lot of respect, but Rex seemed to have gone off the deep end this time. This mission was unlike any of the others Grayson's Guardians had sent him on. To the point that he wasn't sure he'd heard him correctly. "You really want me to be a bodyguard for a rich woman and her seven-year-old kid?"

Rex nodded. The captain was only four years older than Grady's thirty-two, but the grim weariness in his boss's gray eyes betrayed the emotional toil they'd suffered during their last tour in Afghanistan. Grady—he was only Mac to his army buddies—knew that Rex had taken the loss of their teammates hard and that he'd ended up getting divorced after he'd returned stateside. From what Grady could tell, his boss was still grieving. "Yeah, that's exactly what Ms. Lauren Chandler is asking and paying us for. I really need you to do this."

"Why me?" The question popped out before he could stop it. The truth was that someone from the team had to take this assignment. Granted, they were usually sent on rescue or recovery missions. None of them were experts in keeping an eye on a socialite and her daughter.

"Because you have good instincts and even better investigative skills." When his phone dinged, Rex reached for it. "Ms. Chandler has some strong opinions on who she'll accept as her bodyguard. Besides, I have a feeling that we're going to need to work with the police and the FBI on this." Rex held up his phone. "She's here."

Grady swallowed a groan as he rose to his feet. The door to the office swung open, revealing a stunning blonde wearing a long leather coat that probably cost more than his house back in Cody, Wyoming. Lauren Chandler looked rich, even without the sparkly diamond studs in her ears and the expensive-looking clothes. A large leather handbag, which matched her coat, was slung over her shoulder. She looked to be roughly his age. Her pale skin indicated she didn't get out in the sun much, or maybe it was just that it was early February in Chicago. The young girl beside her had long brown hair that was held back from her face with a pink headband, and she had the same brilliant blue eyes as her mother. The little girl also wore a thick navy-blue parka in deference to the freezing-cold Chicago temperatures.

Not unlike Wyoming, he thought with a sigh. No such luck he'd be sent to Florida or some other southern state in the winter.

"Ms. Chandler, this is Mac, er, Grady McFarland. Mac, this is Ms. Lauren Chandler and her daughter, Lucy."

"Nice to meet you." He forced a smile on his face as he stepped forward to offer his hand. To his surprise, Lauren shook it with a firm grip.

"Thanks for agreeing to help me." She glanced at her daughter, and amended, "Help us."

"I was just about to fill Mac in on what's been happening." Rex gestured to the chairs beside his. "Please have a seat."

Lauren removed her leather bag and dropped gracefully into the chair beside his. Her daughter took the seat on her other side, almost as if Lauren had purposefully put herself between him and Lucy. He frowned, not appreciating being viewed as a threat to the little girl.

"A seven-year-old girl was abducted two days ago," Rex said, breaking the silence. "Her name is Ariel Turner, and she happens to be one of Lucy's closest friends. They attend the same private school together."

Grady frowned. "And Ms. Chandler believes that the abduction is an indication Lucy is also in danger?" To his mind, that was a leap, even if Lucy's parents were rich.

"Please, call me Lauren. I have the video on my laptop." She surprised him by removing a computer from her large bag and opening it. "I think when you see this, you'll understand my concern."

Rex inclined his head, indicating she should go ahead with the video. Grady leaned over to see the screen as Lauren queued up the video. A whiff of her perfume teased his senses, but he ignored it. As a client, Lauren was off-limits, even if she wasn't rich and had a daughter. *Three strikes, you're out,* he thought wryly. Besides, he wasn't interested in dating anyone after his former fiancée broke things off. His job caused him to travel across the US, and frankly, he liked the different missions Rex Grayson assigned to them. *Until this most recent request,* he silently amended.

Beside him, Lauren expanded the video on the screen and hit the play button. A young girl wearing a navy-blue parka and a pink headband walked down the sidewalk. She wore white tights beneath a navy blue and green plaid pleated skirt. At first, he thought the girl was Lucy, as they both had brown hair and the same pink headband, but as he searched the girl's facial features, he realized it wasn't.

A man wearing a ski mask suddenly appeared on the screen. He swooped the girl into his arms, covering her mouth with his hand as he darted away. The kidnapping happened so fast Mac blinked in surprise when the short video ended.

"What in the world?" He glanced at Lauren. "Do the police have any leads on who did this? Is there more video that shows the vehicle the kidnapper used to escape?"

"No." Her expression was strained. "The most interesting thing is that Ariel was released less than three hours later." She paused, then added, "After the kidnappers realized they'd grabbed the wrong girl."

A chill snaked down his spine. Okay, now he understood. He caught a glimpse of Lucy's concerned face and framed his comment as carefully as possible. "You believe your daughter is in danger."

Lauren's blue eyes flashed. "I know she is."

"Ariel was scared." Lucy's voice was small. "But the bad man didn't hurt her."

Mac's throat tightened at the thought of Lucy being snatched the same way Ariel had been. He sat up straighter, absorbing the gravity of the situation. "Do Ariel and Lucy always dress alike? I mean, other than wearing their school uniform."

Lauren nodded. "They like to pretend to be twins." Her brow furrowed. "Although not anymore."

"Ariel's mother doesn't like me." Lucy's blue eyes were bright with tears. "She said we can't play together anymore."

"It's okay, Lucy." Lauren wrapped her arm around her daughter's slim shoulders, hugging her close. "Ms. Turner is just upset about what happened. I'm sure that once the bad man is behind bars, everything will go back to normal."

"I hope so." Lucy's voice was muffled against her mother's coat. "Ariel is my best friend."

"I know, sweetie." Lauren's stricken gaze turned to Mac's. "Lucy needs protection. And we also need to understand the source of the threat."

Grady glanced at Rex, then slowly nodded. "I'm sure the local police and the FBI are working on that as well."

"They are, but not with the sense of urgency I expect." Lauren's blue eyes glittered with anger. "Ariel being released has lulled them into complacency. They aren't taking the threat as seriously as I'd like."

He arched a brow at that. When Rex didn't say anything, he nodded. "Okay, let's start with who might have a grudge against you."

Lauren glanced at Lucy, then back at him. "I'd be happy to discuss this at length when we get home."

Grady almost argued, but then realized Lauren didn't want to go into details in front of her daughter. With a resigned sigh, he nodded. "Fine. What's your address? I can meet you there."

She arched a brow. "I'm not leaving without you. My driver dropped us off and escorted us up to the tenth floor. From here, I expect you'll be handling all aspects of our transportation."

She expected him to be her chauffeur? Great. He did his best to hide his annoyance. "I'm driving a Jeep, not a limo."

"I didn't expect a limo." Her tone held a note of disdain. "And there's one more thing we need to discuss."

He glanced again at Rex, who grimaced as if he knew what was coming. He braced himself for the worst. Did she expect him to wear some sort of chauffeur's uniform? Or some other uniform to make sure he blended into the background when she did—whatever rich socialites did?

"I need you to pretend to be my fiancé." Lauren turned to face him. "I don't want the world to know my daughter is in danger."

He blinked. That was so not what he'd expected. "Your fiancé?"

"Yes." A faint blush stained her cheeks. "From what I understand, you're not involved with anyone, correct?" When he managed to nod in agreement, she went on. "Then there's no reason the public in general won't buy our story."

"Except for the fact that we've only seen each other for the first time today," he drawled. Or the fact that he was a former army sergeant from Cody, Wyoming, about as far from the high society page as you could get.

Annoyance flashed in her eyes as she glanced toward Rex. His boss cleared his throat. "Mac, er, Grady will gladly take on the role of your fiancé to keep you and your daughter safe."

He would? Swallowing a flash of irritation, he forced a nod. "Of course. Whatever you think is best."

"Thank you." Satisfied with the arrangement, Lauren rose. She dug a check from her handbag, which doubled as a computer case, and set it on Rex's desk. "For the first week as agreed. I'm hoping you, Grady, and the police are able to figure out who is responsible for abducting Ariel by then."

"Thank you." Rex glanced at the check, then rose. He held out his hand. "Mac, er, Grady will protect you and your daughter with his life."

"I'm counting on it." Lauren's expression was grim as she shook Rex's hand, then turned to him. "Would you like to be called Grady or Mac?"

He cleared his throat. "Grady is fine. It's only my army buddies that call me Mac."

"Fine." She nodded briskly. "Let's go then." She placed her computer in her bag and was about to sling it over her shoulder when he held out his hand. It took a moment for her to realize he intended to carry it for her. "It looks like a purse," she said, clearly flustered by his action.

"That's okay." He didn't care what it looked like, he wasn't about to let her carry it. He shrugged into his leather bomber jacket and took the bag from her hand. "I've got it."

"Thank you." She turned to her daughter. "Let's go, Lucy."

As he followed Lauren and Lucy out of the office, he turned to shoot one last look at Rex. He wasn't the only single agent Rex had working for him. They were all single, although Brody was seeing someone last Grady had heard.

The only reason he was going along with this pretend fiancé/bodyguard deal was the video of the masked man snatching Ariel off the street in broad daylight and knowing Lucy was the intended target.

Rex was right about one thing. He'd protect Lucy and her mother with his life if necessary. Although he grimly hoped it wouldn't come to that.

LAUREN GLANCED FURTIVELY over her shoulder as she stepped out of the office building into the bright sunshine. Her face felt like it might crack from her forced smile. Every nerve ending was on high alert, waiting for the masked man to pop out of the shadows at any moment.

She hadn't slept in the two days since Ariel had been abducted by mistake. And even with hiring a bodyguard, she couldn't relax. One man could only do so much. She'd been tempted to ask for an entire team of bodyguards, but that would only advertise the danger.

"Stay a few feet in front of me." Grady's low, husky voice had her glancing at him. Then just as quickly, she looked away. He was tall, broad-shouldered, and incredibly handsome if you liked rugged-looking men with hair that was too long and needed to be cut.

Which to her dismay, her long-dormant hormones did.

Grady put his arm around her waist, keeping her positioned to his left. She kept Lucy close, then stiffened when she realized Grady held a gun in his right hand.

Well, what did you think? she mentally chided herself. Of course, her bodyguard would be armed with a weapon.

"You're supposed to be my fiancé," she whispered as he directed her to his car. He'd said he drove a Jeep, but somehow she'd expected something with a rag top that he'd use to go four-wheeling in the mountains, not a brand-new Jeep Grand Wagoneer. It was an expensive-looking car. Something she wouldn't mind driving.

"Yeah, but this fiancé plans to be ready for anything." He hustled her to the passenger-side door. "Does Lucy need a booster seat?"

"Technically, yes, but for now, she'll be fine." The booster seat was the least of her worries, although she was a little surprised he'd mentioned it. Most single guys were clueless about that kind of thing. Unless Grady had kids? Whatever. It didn't matter, as long as he did his job.

Except it did matter if he was going to put his life on the line for her. She waited for Lucy to get settled in the back seat, before climbing in herself. When Grady slid in behind the wheel, she asked, "Do you have kids?"

"What? No." He looked startled by her question. "Why do you ask?"

"I was surprised you knew about booster seats."

"I may have grown up in small-town Wyoming, but I didn't live under a rock." His western drawl was back. "I'm friends with a guy who has eight siblings. I'm familiar with what it's like to be around kids."

"I see." She flushed. "I didn't mean any disrespect."

"None taken." He said the words easily, but she sensed his annoyance. She closed her eyes and tried to calm her racing heart. There was no reason to care what Grady McFarland thought about her. He was her bodyguard and fake fiancé. Once this nightmare was over, she'd never see him again.

As he waited for a break in the traffic, she twisted in her seat to look behind them. She hadn't seen anyone suspicious following her and Lucy, but that didn't mean someone wasn't lurking back there, waiting for the opportunity to make his move. The truth was, she had no idea who would want to kidnap Lucy.

The motive had to be money because that was the only thing that made sense. She hadn't mentioned how she'd been kidnapped once as a child, after her father had made the news as the first Chicago billionaire. Granted, that was twenty-five years ago, when she was about Lucy's age.

That her daughter would be targeted in the same way bothered her. She'd cooperated with the police and FBI investigation and had racked her brain for a list of suspects. But as far as she could tell, the police were no closer to finding this guy.

Which did not bode well for Lucy.

"I'll need your address," Grady said, interrupting her thoughts.

She rattled off the building number, then gestured to the skyscraper looming to the right. It looked closer than it actually was. "It's the black building behind that one. It's called Savion Enterprises. We live in the penthouse apartment."

"Underground parking I presume?" He glanced at her.

"Yes." She wasn't sure why Grady made her feel nervous. If anything, it should be the other way around. She had been born and raised here in the Windy City of Chicago, and he was a fish out of water. Or he should have been, except that he carried himself with an air of confidence that she envied.

Then again, his child wasn't the intended target of a kidnapping for ransom. She and Lucy were just another job for him. Her father had recommended Grayson's Guardians when she'd asked him for advice. Apparently, Rex Grayson was some sort of war hero who had led a team in combat. A team who had all earned bronze stars for their bravery under fire.

She'd jumped at the opportunity of having someone with battle experience protecting her daughter. Now that she was sitting there beside Grady, doubts pummeled her.

He looked competent enough, but she hadn't anticipated his being so—big. Muscular. Rugged. Strong.

She put a hand to her throbbing temple and told herself to stop being ridiculous. Her lack of sleep was getting to her.

"Are you hungry?" Grady's question caught her by surprise. "I'm happy to stop and grab something if you'd like."

"No thanks. Clara, our housekeeper, probably has dinner cooking by now."

"Okay." If he was surprised to hear she had a housekeeper, he didn't show it. "Do you know anything else about the vehicle used in the abduction?"

"The car was a black SUV." His Jeep was black too. "I believe it was a Honda."

His green gaze flicked to the rearview mirror, then back at her. "Lots of black SUVs on the road."

Her heart thumped painfully against her sternum. She twisted in her seat again to look through the back window. "Do you see something suspicious?"

"Just stating a fact." His calm demeanor did not make her feel any better. "Traffic is so congested here that it's hard to spot a tail. That's why I was thinking it would be good to stop and get food. See if the two black SUVs behind us stick around or keep going."

"Mom? Is the bad man back there?" The fear underscoring Lucy's tone wrenched at her heart. No child should be afraid of being kidnapped.

"I don't think so, sweetie. Mr.—ah, Grady is just being cautious." She flashed him a pointed look. "Right?"

"Right." Grady made eye contact with her daughter. "Don't worry. Nothing bad is going to happen while I'm around, okay?"

"Okay." Lucy's tremulous smile tugged at her heart. Having divorced Nelson five years ago and obtaining sole custody of Lucy, she knew her daughter didn't have any memories of her father. Since Nelson was in jail for manslaughter, Lauren preferred to keep it that way. How she'd been so blind to Nelson's dark side, she had no idea.

Maybe it was wrong to be glad Nelson was in jail. Their divorce had been contentious despite the prenup she'd required him to sign. She'd soon learned Nelson had only married her because of her wealth.

Whatever. That was old news. As much as she could easily envision Nelson doing something as low as abducting his own daughter for a hefty ransom, he was in jail. And therefore, he couldn't be responsible.

Someone else was behind this. Too bad the list of suspects pretty much included everyone who resented the wealthy.

"I changed my mind. Let's stop for pizza." Once the idea took hold in her mind, she couldn't let it go. She glanced at Grady. "You can have whatever you like, but we need to order one pepperoni pizza for Lucy."

"Really? Pepperoni pizza?" Lucy sounded excited. "Yay!"

A reluctant smile tugged at the corner of her mouth as she glanced back at her daughter. "We'll have to blame Grady for wanting pizza so Clara doesn't get upset with us."

"Oh yeah?" Grady's wry drawl made her glance at him to see if he was truly upset. The twinkle in his green eyes indicated he wasn't. "Sure, make me the bad guy right out of the gate."

"It's just that she fusses over us and takes it personally when we don't eat what she's prepared." Lauren shrugged. "Normally, that's not a problem, as I prefer to serve Lucy healthy meals."

"Healthy is fine, but this is a special occasion," Grady said. When she frowned in confusion, he rolled his eyes. "Our engagement! Surely you haven't forgotten our engagement already."

She blushed at his teasing. The people around her tended to cater to whatever she wanted. Which, quite frankly, got old fast. She wasn't used to being teased.

"Of course, I didn't forget. That's a great excuse for us to use." She decided not to point out that if they were truly engaged, they'd be celebrating with steak, lobster, and champagne. For a moment, she envied Grady's simpler lifestyle. Then she gave herself a mental shake. There was no point in wishing for something else. She'd been given many blessings. And she'd made it her mission to champion various charity events. Her favorite by far was the work she did as the spokesperson for St. Mary's Children's Hospital in Chicago. When Lucy had been born, she'd needed emergency open heart surgery. From that point forward, Lauren had made it her mission to make sure all children received the care they needed, regardless of their ability to pay.

Thankfully, she was in a position to make that happen. Not only were her parents wealthy, but her father's parents had left her a large trust fund. A fund that Nelson had hoped to get his hands on.

The jerk.

"What's your favorite pizza place?" Grady asked, interrupting her thoughts.

"Um." She didn't want to admit that when they ordered pizza, Clara took care of the details.

"I like Captain Jack's pizza," Lucy announced. "That's the kind Ariel's parents get from the store."

Grady shot her a quizzical look, probably wondering what kind of world her daughter lived in. "Any pizza you think looks good is fine with us," she hastily added.

"Got it." He made an abrupt turn to the right. She braced herself with a hand on the dashboard when she heard a loud crack.

Confused, she looked around, wondering if someone had gotten in a car crash.

"Down!" Grady shoved her head down as he drove the Jeep up and over a curb. The jarring motion made her teeth snap together.

"Mommy?" Lucy's plaintive voice had her turning to

look at her daughter. When she noticed the rear window was shattered, she belatedly realized the banging sound wasn't a car crash.

It was gunfire!

2

———

Mentally kicking himself for not being better prepared, Grady recklessly drove up and over the curb to get off the traffic-packed street. After driving through a narrow alley, Grady went down another curb, forcing two cars to stop so he could merge into traffic heading the opposite way. Ignoring the blaring of horns—Chicago drivers used them often regardless of annoying driving—he managed to put more distance between his Jeep and the black SUV that had taken shots at them.

"Lucy, are you okay?" Lauren's voice trembled with concern. "You're not cut by glass, are you?"

"No." The little girl sniffled and wiped at her face with her mitten. "I'm scared."

"I know you are, sweetie." Lauren turned to look at him. "Did you get a good look at the car?"

He shook his head, the bitter taste of failure coating his tongue. Less than thirty minutes into their time together and he'd almost gotten them killed. So much for being a good bodyguard. "It was a black SUV with tinted windows.

The cars were so close together I didn't get a good look at the front end to identify a make or model. Much less a license plate." He risked a quick glance at Lauren, before turning his attention back to the street. He forced his Jeep into the next lane of traffic so that he could get off the main thoroughfare sooner rather than later.

No doubt Lauren would call Rex to let him know she wanted someone else assigned to her case. He honestly couldn't blame her.

For now, he needed to get them to safety. Their plan of stopping for pizza was not happening. He felt bad for Lucy, who'd seemed enthusiastic about having pepperoni pizza for dinner.

It had been foolish of him to think he could do something so mundane as stopping for something to eat.

He took another right-hand turn, then wedged his Jeep across the next lane of traffic to turn left at the next intersection. More horns blared at his aggressive driving.

For a moment, he wished they were in Cody, Wyoming. He was more familiar with his hometown compared to the maze of skyscrapers and narrow side streets he navigated around now.

"Do you mind if I turn up the heat for Lucy?" Lauren's soft-spoken question surprised him. He'd anticipated she'd be screaming at him for allowing this to happen. Maybe she was holding back until they were safe.

"Of course not." He pressed a button to increase the heat blowing from the vents. "I'm sorry about this. We'll be at your building soon."

"I understand." Her voice was strained. She turned in her seat to face her daughter. "I'm sorry, Lucy. We won't get to have pizza tonight after all. But I'll make sure we can order out for pizza tomorrow."

"Okay." Lucy's small voice tugged at his heart. Grady hadn't wanted this case, but handing Lauren and Lucy off to one of the other guys didn't sit well with him.

Not that he would have much choice in the matter.

Taking side streets, he managed to get closer to the black skyscraper, Savion Enterprises. He searched for the entrance to the underground parking garage.

"It's on the other side of the building," Lauren said, reading his mind.

"Thanks." He threaded his Jeep through traffic to circle the building. When he finally got to the entrance, he was stopped by the gate. The barrier was thick and heavy enough to prevent anyone from ramming through.

A man in his mid-fifties, bundled in a thick black coat and hat against the cold weather, stared at him through the window of an enclosed booth. Grady lowered his window, then leaned back so the guy could see Lauren.

"Hi, Trent, it's me and Lucy. This is Grady McFarland, my fiancé. We just got into a fender-bender accident." The explanation for the shattered rear window was weak, but Grady didn't say anything to contradict her. "Please let us through."

"Sure thing, Ms. Lauren." If Trent was suspicious of the fender-bender story, he didn't let on. "Nice to meet you, Mr. Grady, and congrats on your engagement." Trent pressed a button to lift the heavy gate. Grady didn't waste any time driving through.

"You shouldn't have introduced me as your fiancé." Grady glanced at Lauren as he drove through the parking garage. "That's going to make it harder to replace me with someone else."

She frowned. "Why would I replace you?"

He risked a glance at Lucy in the back seat. She looked

calmer now that they were off the street. He kept his voice low. "Because I failed you. Which reminds me, we need to notify the police about the shooting attempt. That's very different from kidnapping."

Lauren shrugged, then gestured to the right. "We have preferred parking over there. See the Porsche? Pull into the spot beside it."

Seeing the white Porsche, he pulled in beside it. The fact that Lauren hadn't instantly fired him was a surprise. He'd expected her to be demanding and somewhat unreasonable.

She was proving to be neither.

He killed the engine and quickly pushed out of the car. He opened the back door for Lucy, then went around to the passenger side for Lauren. She had her oversized laptop bag slung over her shoulder, and since he had already underestimated the danger once, he decided to keep both his hands free in the event they stumbled across another threat.

Removing his gun from its holster, he carried it pointed down at the ground in his right hand, resting his left in the small of Lauren's back. He scanned their surroundings, not liking the fact that there were so many cars parked on this level.

Too many places for a gunman to hide. Despite the security guard, Trent, Grady felt certain sneaking into the structure wouldn't be that difficult.

"Stay close," he murmured as he steered Lauren and Lucy to the elevator vestibule. The clear glass walls made it easy to see that the area was empty.

Once they were inside the glass enclosure, Lauren rummaged in her bag. She pulled out a small keycard that she used to summon the elevator.

Less than a minute later, they were inside. Lauren's key card worked on the inside panel, too, and they headed straight up to the penthouse level without stopping. *Thirty-six floors*, he thought wryly. As security went, it was decent.

"Wait." He held his arm out to keep Lauren and Lucy inside the elevator until he could look around. The penthouse apartment sported two white double doors. There were no other doorways in sight.

Personally, he couldn't imagine living in such a place, but his opinion of Lauren's lifestyle didn't matter. He stood to the side as Lauren used the key card to unlock the door.

"The same keycard works on the elevator and the main entrance?" He frowned as he stepped across the threshold behind her. "It would be better to have two different key cards."

Lauren frowned at him over her shoulder, then turned to Lucy. "I'll take your coat. Why don't you run and let Clara know we'll have a guest for dinner?" Lauren smiled as she ran her hand over her daughter's silky hair. "Grady and I need to talk for a few minutes, okay?"

"Okay." Lucy glanced at him, then turned to do her mother's bidding.

Lauren shrugged out of her leather coat, then proceeded to hang them in the hall closet. He reached past her for a hanger to do the same.

"Please, have a seat." Lauren led the way into a large sitting room that was bigger than his entire house. The entire wall of windows offered a breathtaking view of Lake Michigan. The buttery soft tan leather furniture was surprisingly comfortable, and he eyed the baby grand piano in the corner of the room with interest. Did Lauren play? Or was Lucy taking lessons? The décor of the penthouse apartment was plush, and he found himself examining the soles of his sturdy boots to make sure he hadn't dragged dirt and debris inside.

This place was about as far from Cody, Wyoming, as a person could get, but he kept his thoughts to himself. Instead, he watched Lauren. She looked a little nervous now as she dropped onto the sofa beside him, crossing one black-clad leg over the other.

"I'm not replacing you. It's probably my fault that the kidnapper knew where to find us. He must have followed my limo driver to the office building." She grimaced, then added, "I know you have questions about who is behind the abduction. The person who would normally be on the top of my suspect list is my ex-husband, Nelson Derringer, but it just so happens he's serving a seven-year stint for manslaughter and still has two more years to go before he's eligible for parole."

The news surprised him. "Who did he kill?"

"His best friend, Bobby, er, Robert Morton." A flicker of distaste flashed in her blue eyes. "Bobby and Nelson were in the same college fraternity at Loyola. Nelson was driving under the influence, and since that was his second offense, and the fact that Bobby died in the crash, the judge threw the book at him."

"I take it that worked out well for you in the divorce."

"Yes, but we were already separated, and I had a solid prenup. Nelson wasn't going to get a dime no matter what." She stared down at her hands for a long moment, then looked up at him. "Nelson is the reason I wanted you to play my fiancé. He's sent numerous letters from prison. I read the first few, thinking maybe I could save them for Lucy, but all he did was beg me to take him back. And he never once mentioned our daughter."

"Lucy is better off without him." Grady made a mental note to dig into her ex-husband's background. Even from jail, the guy could have hired someone to go after Lucy.

"That's correct." Her blue eyes hardened. "He hasn't seen her since she was a baby, and I plan to keep it that way."

"So you want Nelson to believe you've moved on with someone else." He held her gaze. "What happens when the kidnapper is found and we're no longer a couple?"

"I'll figure something out." She waved that off. "The charade is not just for Nelson, but for other men who seem to think I might be interested. It's a bit of a meat market out there."

He could only imagine how men trailed after her. She was beautiful, rich, and likely seen as the hottest bachelorette in the city. "Okay, that's fine."

"As far as Lucy goes, I was granted full custody after the drunk-driving accident." She shrugged. "The truth is that other than Nelson, I can't think of anyone who would want to kidnap Lucy for ransom. Unless it's some stranger, which will make him more difficult to find."

"And you're convinced ransom is the ultimate goal?"

Lauren frowned. "Yes, why else? Oh, you mean like sex trafficking?" She shook her head. "No reason to let Ariel go if that was the case. Besides, people who tend to kidnap kids for something like that look for easy targets. Not kids of wealthy parents."

She had a point, so he nodded. "Okay, we'll operate under the assumption someone wants to grab Lucy for money. Have the police fully vetted your house staff? Clara and whoever else you have helping you?"

"We have Clara, who has a key to get in and out of the penthouse. The rest of the staff, security guards like Trent, are hired by my father to keep the building secure. They've all worked here for years, hard to imagine any of them are involved."

"Your father owns this building?" That surprised him.

He'd grossly underestimated the magnitude of Lauren's wealth. A building like this had to be worth a hundred million or more. It was a staggering amount of money. No wonder she'd assumed the goal was ransom. A kidnapper could ask for ten million without putting a dent in her father's pocketbook.

"Yes. This building along with others." She shifted on the sofa cushion to face him. "I have two charity events on Friday and Saturday. Lucy is upset that I won't let her attend school until we catch this guy, but I think she needs to stick close to me where it's safe."

"Why not just cancel your charity events?" He didn't understand why she would risk going out. "You could stay here with Lucy. I'll work as a liaison with the local police and/or the FBI to make sure they continue their investigation." The thought of doing that was far more appealing than showing up at her side for some silly dinner.

"February is Heart Month for St. Mary's Children's Hospital. It's important for me to raise money for them." She lifted her chin, eyeing him stubbornly. "They were amazing when Lucy needed open heart surgery a year after she was born. I currently have pledges for over five million dollars to support families in need. I expect that by Friday that amount could be doubled. Canceling the event isn't an option. I'm attending, no matter what."

He stifled a sigh. Okay, maybe it was for a good cause. He still didn't think it was worth the risk. "What about having someone else stay here to watch Lucy?"

"I've considered that." Lauren bit her lower lip. "I think it's best if Lucy comes with me. We need to stick together."

Grady didn't necessarily agree, but since he didn't have a choice, he nodded in agreement.

Despite the luxurious surroundings, he grimly realized

that keeping Lauren and Lucy safe would not be as easy as it sounded.

And he could only hope that he didn't fail them again.

LAUREN WAS FAR TOO aware of Grady sitting beside her. Why she found him attractive, she had no idea. Nelson had proven she had lousy taste in men, and she wasn't going to go out with anyone who might be looking for easy money.

"You mentioned calling the police." She glanced at her watch. "I think we should wait until after dinner. I'll ask Lieutenant Olson to come here to meet with us."

"That's fine. In the meantime, I need you to think hard about who else might be holding a grudge against you." Grady's expression was grim. "It could be someone with a beef against your father since he's the one with the money."

"I have a trust fund, too, but you're right in that my father is worth more than I am. And of course, he would pay a ransom to get Lucy back." She glanced over when Clara entered the room. "I'll make a list for you after dinner." She rose. "Clara, this is my fiancé, Grady McFarland. Grady, I'd like you to meet Clara. She's been with us since before Lucy was born."

"Nice to meet you." He rose and crossed the room to shake her hand. "Something smells good."

"Nice to meet you too. Dinner is ready, Ms. Lauren." Clara quickly turned to leave.

"I hope you like grilled swordfish," she murmured, leading the way into the dining room. "If you have any food allergies or strong dislikes, you should probably let me know."

"I'm not picky. Swordfish sounds great." He grinned,

then added, "Although I can see why Lucy wanted pepperoni pizza. I didn't have swordfish until I was an adult."

She sighed, knowing he was probably right. But she didn't care. She wanted Lucy to experience a variety of healthy foods. "She had open heart surgery as a baby."

The smile faded from his eyes. "I can only imagine how difficult that was for you."

"Hence the healthy diet." In the dining room, she took the seat next to her daughter, indicating Grady should sit across from them. "My father is out of town on business for the week, or he'd have joined us."

"Okay." Grady held her gaze for a moment, then folded his hands in his lap and bowed his head. It took a moment for her to realize he was praying. She hastily looked away, wondering if he was putting on a show for her benefit. Then she realized there was no reason for him to do that. Despite their pretend engagement, once this kidnapper was caught, they wouldn't see each other again.

She didn't know anyone who prayed before meals. She'd spent a lot of time in the hospital chapel while Lucy had been a baby undergoing surgery, but this was different.

Clara interrupted the moment by bringing in a tray of food. Along with the grilled swordfish, there was roasted asparagus and parmesan-crusted red potatoes. After setting the various platters on the table, Clara stepped back. "Would you like anything else, Ms. Lauren?"

"No, but thanks, Clara. Everything looks delicious." The adults had water, while Lucy had a glass of milk. She glanced at Grady, wondering if he wanted something else. "We have soft drinks if you prefer." She didn't serve alcohol at meals.

"I'm fine with water. And yes, this looks amazing." Grady

smiled at Clara in a way that made the older woman blush. "Thanks."

"I wanna go to school tomorrow," Lucy said once they'd started eating. "I miss my friends. Especially Ariel."

"Maybe next week." Lauren kept the timeline vague. "Mrs. Poole sent your assignments home, so you can work on those tomorrow."

Lucy's lower lip trembled. "That's not the same. I wanna go to school."

She glanced at Grady, who had dug in to his meal with relish. His comment about pepperoni pizza aside, he appeared to be enjoying the swordfish. He surprised her by sending Lucy a stern look. "You need to listen to your mother. She's only keeping you home from school because she's worried about you."

Lucy bent her head and picked at her food. "I don't care. I'd run so fast the bad guy couldn't get me."

Swallowing a sigh, she gave Grady a nod of gratitude for his support. One minute Lucy was scared of the masked man, the next she made comments like that. "You can video chat with Ellie after dinner."

Lucy stabbed a piece of fish and ate it. "Okay, but that's not the same as going to school either."

Tomorrow was Thursday, and the kidnapping of Ariel Turner had been on Tuesday. Keeping Lucy home wasn't unreasonable, but logic didn't mean much to a kid. "Grady, tell us what it's like to live in Wyoming," she said, anxious to change the subject. "We've never been there."

"It's cold, like it is here. We have a lot of snow too. Ours comes in from the mountains; yours is impacted by Lake Michigan. But we don't have big skyscrapers like this." Grady gestured to their surroundings. "Our tallest building is a hotel that's three stories high. The windows overlooking

Lake Michigan are nice, but we have a view of snowcapped mountains and forests outside our windows. They're pretty impressive."

"I'm sure they're beautiful." She'd skied down the mountains of Switzerland but hadn't visited Wyoming. Strangely, she felt bad about that. Maybe she should make a point of taking Lucy to visit more of the states that made up their home.

"I own a small house in Cody," Grady went on. "I've considered selling since I don't spend a lot of time there, but it's nice to have a home base." A wry grin tugged at the corner of his mouth. "My friends, the Sullivans, have been using it in my absence. They've kindly fixed the damage they'd inadvertently caused."

"Damage?" Imagining wild parties, she shook her head. "That's rude."

"Oh, they didn't damage the place on purpose. Only because they happened to be in danger and kept getting found." He glanced at Lucy, then hastily added, "They're fine now, though. No injuries or other problems."

"I see." Except she really didn't. It seemed strange that his friends would borrow his house while knowing they were in danger. She couldn't imagine doing something like that here. She'd heard rumors of lack of lawlessness while living in the Wild West, but she had assumed they were grossly exaggerated.

Apparently not.

She'd thought Grady's military experience would come in handy. Maybe his life in Wyoming had contributed to his confidence too.

When they'd finished eating, she told Lucy to take her dishes into the kitchen before she made her video call. Lucy sighed dramatically but did as she was told.

Grady rose to stack his plate too. "Oh, you don't need to do that," she said.

"House rules." He winked and carried his dishes into the kitchen. Flustered, she followed. Grady didn't act like most men she knew. Maybe it was his western upbringing.

When the table was cleared, she watched as Clara pulled on her coat. "Did you need anything else, Ms. Lauren?"

"No, thanks, Clara. Have a good evening."

After seeing Clara to the door, she pulled out her phone to call Lieutenant Olson. He answered on the first ring. "Ms. Chandler? Is everything okay?"

"Not exactly. I, uh, need to report another incident that involves me and my good friend. I'd like you and Detective Kramer to come here to take a report." She'd planned to introduce Grady as her fiancé, but now she realized that was more difficult than she'd anticipated. She hadn't been seeing anyone when she'd met with Lieutenant Olson and Detective Kramer the day before. Lying didn't come easily to her, but she pressed forward. "His name is Grady McFarland. He's in town from Cody, Wyoming."

"I didn't realize you had a friend visiting from out of town," Lieutenant Olson said. "We need to make sure he's not involved."

"He's not. But you can speak with him about that yourself." She hoped the police would take her statement about being engaged at face value. She'd call the chief of police if necessary but decided to hold off for now.

"Barry Kramer and I will be there in twenty minutes," Lieutenant Olson said. "And trust me, I will run your friend through the system."

She barely refrained from rolling her eyes. If he wanted to spin his wheels, that was fine with her. "Thanks. We'll see you soon." She closed her eyes for a moment and then tossed her phone onto the table. "This is getting complicated."

Grady arched a brow. "You're the one who wanted to be engaged. We can stick with the *we're just friends* angle if that's easier."

"No, this is better. Especially for the two charity events." She forced a smile. Maybe it was selfish, but she was glad to have Grady attending the dinners with her as her fiancé. That should keep the jackals at bay, at least for a while. "I'll arrange for a tux to be delivered."

He shrugged but didn't argue. "It's more important that I pick out a ring."

"Oh, well." She flushed. "Don't worry about that."

"We'll say it's being sized for now." Grady arched a brow. "But without a ring, nobody will take this seriously."

Her head started to ache, mostly from the lack of sleep. She hated to admit he was right. "I'll get a ring. In the meantime, I'll show you to your room. I, uh, don't know if you have much in the way of luggage."

"Just a carry-on in my Jeep. I'll grab it later." He stood. "Show me where you and Lucy will be too."

"Of course." She led the way down the hall to the bedrooms. The master suite was on the other side of the penthouse apartment, where her father stayed when he was in town. "This is my room, and it's next to Lucy's." She pointed to the door hanging ajar. Her daughter was already chatting with Ellie. "This is the guest room. Sorry to say the view isn't as nice." She didn't know why she was apologizing. Grady wasn't there for the view.

"It's great, thanks." He tucked his thumbs into the front pockets of his jeans. "I'll need one of your keycards."

"Of course." She ducked into her room to grab it. "Here you go."

The intercom buzzed from the living room. She crossed over to answer.

"Detective Kramer is here." The lobby attendant informed her.

"Please send him up, thanks." She turned to Grady. "He must have been close by."

Grady frowned and stood beside her. When she moved forward to answer the door, he held her arm and stepped forward to use the peephole. Then he opened the door. "Detective, I'm Grady McFarland."

"Nice to meet you." Detective Kramer turned to face her. "I was surprised to hear you wanted to talk to us, because it just so happens I planned to talk to you too. We have a man in custody by the name of Jorge Dombach. We think he's the kidnapper."

"Really?" Her jaw dropped in surprise. "The name doesn't sound familiar."

"When did you arrest him?" Grady asked.

Detective Kramer frowned at him. "Who are you again?"

"Grady McFarland, a longtime friend and new fiancé of Lauren's." Grady didn't flinch. "I really need to know when you arrested this guy."

"At four thirty this afternoon," Detective Kramer said. "I would have been here sooner, but we've been trying to get him to cooperate. Unfortunately, he's not saying much."

Grady shook his head in disgust. Lauren understood why he was annoyed. Clearly, Jorge Dombach, whoever he might be, wasn't the kidnapper.

And she was beginning to doubt the Chicago PD was capable of finding the man who was.

3

———

"He's not our guy, unless he's working with someone else." Grady held the detective's gaze. "Someone in a black SUV followed us from an office building downtown and fired shots at us. That was between five fifteen and five thirty this evening."

"Shots?" Kramer frowned. "Why would the kidnapper change his MO? Maybe we have the kidnapper and the shooter is someone else."

"Both using black SUVs?" Lauren shook her head. "I don't think so. I believe I may have been followed when I went to our, uh, appointment."

Grady understood she was trying to avoid telling Kramer that she'd gone to meet with his boss to hire him as her bodyguard. He reached for her hand, in what he hoped was a concerned-fiancé type of gesture. "I agree with Lauren, this guy must have been keeping an eye on the building and managed to follow us as we got into my Jeep." There was no other way the kidnapper could have known Grady would be with Lauren and Lucy. He hadn't even known what case his boss had assigned to him.

"What makes you think this Jorge Dombach is the kidnapper?"

Kramer scowled, as if annoyed to learn about the shooting that had ruined his theory. "We spotted a black SUV on a traffic cam about a mile from the site of the kidnapping. He has a criminal record for drug possession and robbery."

"Can we see the video of his SUV?" Lauren squeezed his hand, as if thanking him for being there. "Maybe Grady can tell if it's similar to the one that shot at us."

"Yeah, I guess." Kramer still looked disgruntled as he pulled out his phone. Then he held the device toward Grady. He released Lauren's hand to take it, moving closer to her and holding the screen so they could both watch the traffic cam video.

The SUV in question was an older model Honda, with a large dent in the back bumper. It looked to him as if the paint was scraped off the rear portion of the roof of the car too. He suspected there were other dings and dents on the vehicle, but the angle of the camera was such that they could only see the back and part of the roof as the driver passed through the light. He shook his head and handed the phone back. "I don't think he's our guy."

"Based on what?" Kramer demanded.

"You mentioned witnesses saw a black SUV at the scene of the kidnapping. I think they'd have noticed if there were dents in the car. And the vehicle I saw behind me had tinted windows and looked new. This one doesn't."

"Maybe Dombach is working with someone else." Kramer clearly didn't want to believe they were on the wrong path. "He's being arraigned in the morning. We're going to ask the judge to hold him without bail because he's a danger to children."

He shrugged and glanced at Lauren. "That's up to you. But I don't think you should stop investigating other suspects."

Kramer scowled again and pocketed his phone. "How many shots were fired?"

"Only one, which I thought was strange at the time." Looking back, Grady wondered why the gunman hadn't fired several shots, barraging his Jeep with bullets. "He took out the rear window. I have my Jeep parked down in the parking garage if you'd like to see the damage for yourself."

Before Kramer could answer, the intercom buzzed. Lauren walked over to answer the summons. "Yes, please send Lieutenant Olson up. Thank you." She turned to look at him. "We may as well wait until the lieutenant arrives. Then we can take them both down to the parking garage."

"Fine with me." He'd snag his overnight bag while they were down there, although he doubted he'd get much sleep. Being in the army had taught him to fall asleep just about anywhere, but he couldn't afford to let his guard down while protecting Lauren and Lucy.

Despite the seemingly tight security, he wasn't convinced that staying in a penthouse apartment with only one way out via an elevator ride or a zillion stairs was the best option.

Lauren opened the door to let the lieutenant in. The two cops exchanged a look before the lieutenant turned toward him. "You heard about our arrest?"

"Yeah. Did you know that someone in a new black SUV with tinted windows shot at us at between five fifteen and five thirty, well after that arrest?" He gestured to Lauren, getting the sense she was annoyed at how the men deferred to him, rather than addressing her. "We've looked at the traffic cam video. I understand why you grabbed this

Dombach guy, his criminal record makes him a good suspect, but I don't think he's responsible."

"Why would a kidnapper decide to shoot at your vehicle?" Olson asked.

"Good question." He'd wondered about the change in MO too. "My best guess is that he figured he'd disable us long enough to make an attempt to get Lucy."

"Let's head down to the parking garage." Lauren looked as if she wanted both of the police to finish their report and get out of there. "It's been a long day, and I'm exhausted."

He hesitated, glancing back at the bedrooms. "Maybe Lucy should come with us."

Lauren nodded and quickly went to get her daughter. Lucy glanced at the cops with interest, but she didn't complain as they all headed out to the elevator and down to the parking garage.

Lieutenant Olson frowned when he saw the shattered rear window of his Jeep. "Looks as if the gunman was aiming for you, McFarland."

"I know. And that's why I think your guy isn't the kidnapper. It seems more logical the gunman's goal was to eliminate me from the picture to have access to Lauren and Lucy." Even as he said the words, he realized that Lauren might be a target now too. Kidnapping a mother and daughter would increase the value of a ransom demand. And it would help the kidnappers to have the mother caring for the child.

Detective Kramer took pictures of his damaged Jeep, then turned to the lieutenant. "I think we continue to hold Dombach for a few days. Maybe he saw something since he was so close to the scene of the kidnapping."

Grady opened the back of the Jeep to grab his duffel. He'd need to get the glass replaced very soon. He decided to call Rex Grayson in the morning to make the arrangements.

As Lauren spoke with the two police officers, he scanned the parking garage. There were way too many cars for him to memorize any license plates. He pulled out his phone and took a video of the cars in the general vicinity of his Jeep and the white Porsche that he assumed belonged to Lauren.

He pocketed his phone and followed the rest as they headed to the elevator. Lucy was unusually quiet as the rode to the penthouse.

Outside the apartment door, Lauren turned to the lieutenant and detective. "Thank you for coming out to update us on your progress and to hear about the gunfire incident. I would appreciate being in the loop moving forward. Grady will be staying here with us."

The lieutenant sized him up. "I ran your background, it's clean. But tell me again how you and Ms. Chandler met?"

"Through mutual friends." He nodded at both men. "Thanks again, please excuse us. It's getting late, and Lucy needs to get some sleep."

And just like that, Lauren had opened the apartment, ushering Lucy inside and closing the door on the Chicago police before they could ask more questions. She arched a brow. "What mutual friends exactly?"

He shrugged. "You tell me. Maybe someone who attended one of your charity events."

She thought about that for a moment. "My friend Suzanne and her husband, Eli White. They've been to Wyoming to ski. We'll say that you somehow met with them there and introduced us."

He filed the names away in his memory. Then he glanced at Lucy who hovered near her mom. "Are you doing okay?"

She nodded, but her expression was wary. "I'm afraid I'll have nightmares," she confided.

"I'll be right across the hall if you do." He dropped to one knee so he could look the little girl in the eye. "Nobody will get to you as long as I'm here, okay?"

Lucy nodded, her dark hair falling partially over her face. "Okay."

"Come, Lucy, time to get ready for bed." Lauren flashed a grateful smile as she led her daughter down the hall. "We're safe here. There's no reason to be afraid."

Grady watched them go, then moved toward the wide double doors that led into the hallway and elevator vestibule. There were deadbolt locks on the door, but he still didn't love the set up. Interesting that Clara didn't live on-site, but maybe she preferred it that way.

He headed to a short hallway that led to the master suite. There was a decent-sized living area in addition to a large bedroom and full-sized bathroom. Again, the main bedroom had a stunning view of Lake Michigan. Shaking his head at the extravagance of the place, he returned to the living room.

Lauren joined him a few minutes later. "I hope Lucy doesn't have nightmares. I feel bad for her. Children shouldn't have to live in fear of being kidnapped."

"I know, but we'll keep her safe." He gestured for Lauren to sit. "I really need you to make a list of anyone who could remotely be involved."

"I've started one," she admitted. "But I think this is the work of some stranger who thinks they deserve easy money."

"That's possible, but don't you think this guy is more likely someone you or your father knows?"

She frowned, appearing lost in thought, before she

looked up at him. "Twenty-five years ago, I was kidnapped from school by a man named Jerry Cromwell who had recently lost his job and decided he deserved to be wealthy. Things weren't as electronic back then, but the FBI did try to trace his calls. My father paid the million-dollar ransom demand, and I was released as promised. I know most cases don't end well, but mine did."

He stared at her in shock. "I had no idea you were kidnapped as a child."

"Yeah, well, that was a long time ago." Lauren tucked her blond hair behind her ear. "The point is, this guy almost got away with it. The police grilled me for hours about where we were and what the man looked like. He didn't use a face mask, like the guy who'd taken Ariel. I was able to give a reasonable description with the help of a sketch artist. A week later, the FBI caught him as he was boarding a plane to Florida."

"I'm glad they caught him." Grady's heart twisted at how frightened she must have been. Not just during the kidnapping, but afterward. It would've been a harrowing experience that had to be difficult to recover from. "Is Cromwell still in jail?"

"I believe so." She shrugged. "If not, he's too old to be involved in this incident. He was thirty-five at the time, which makes him sixty now. The man we saw on video moved quickly enough that I anticipate he's much younger than that."

"Age alone doesn't preclude someone staying in shape," he pointed out. "And sixty isn't that old. People that age are still running marathons. Some men use being in jail to get into shape. Cromwell could have done that too. We need to make sure he's still in jail."

"Maybe." She sighed. "I can add his name to the list. My

only reason for telling you the story was that I didn't know Jerry prior to his taking me from school, and neither did my father. This was a case where he'd caught something about us on the news and decided to use me to get rich."

He nodded. It would be far easier if she had made someone mad, like her ex-husband or someone else, but she had a point about the suspect being anyone who needed what they perceived as easy cash. "I haven't had time to research the statistics on kidnapping to know what we're dealing with."

"The child abduction rate by a stranger is very low, less than two percent of all abductions." She grimaced. "However, that number is skewed a little higher when wealthy people are targeted. The good news is that most kidnappings for ransom have a high success rate of the child being recovered." Her smile was strained. "Like in my case. It's the creepy pedophiles that are far more dangerous."

He reached for her hand. "I'm sorry you had to go through that."

"Thanks. Although it could have been worse." She tightened her hand on his. "The charity event on Saturday night is to fight human trafficking, especially of women and children. I know it takes more than money, but I've funneled a lot of funds to various organizations who work on recovering those victims and supporting them afterward. It's another cause that's near and dear to my heart."

He nodded slowly. His opinion of Lauren being a socialite who spent her days at the spa was changing by the second. She might be rich, living in a fancy penthouse apartment, but she was doing her part in tackling the world's problems. In her own way, which was more than most people did, he thought wryly. "That's a very worthy cause."

"Yes." She gazed at their clasped hands for a moment, then pulled free and stood. "Well, I need to finish my list of suspects. You should get some sleep."

He rose. "I'll stay out here for a while. Your father isn't expected to return home later tonight, is he?"

"No, he has business in New York through the weekend. Good night, Grady. Thanks again for being here."

"Of course." He found it odd that Lauren's father would go on a business trip while knowing his granddaughter was targeted by a kidnapper. Then again, he didn't know that much about the relationship between the three of them. "Lauren, what happened to your mother?"

"She passed away fifteen years ago from cancer." She managed a smile. "Pancreatic cancer from smoking. Cancer research is another charity we support, even though in my mother's case, her cancer was related to her lifestyle choices."

"I'm sorry for your loss." His own parents were retired and living in Arizona, far away from the harsh winters of Wyoming.

"Thank you. Good night." She turned and headed for her room.

He stood for a moment in the living room that was larger than his house and thought about what she'd said. Stranger abductions were rare, but he knew they couldn't afford to discount the possibility.

But if that was the case, it would take a miracle to find the person responsible without something more to go on.

He could only hope and pray that this kidnapper would slip up along the way, giving them the opportunity to find and arrest him.

∼

LAUREN RACKED her brain for names to add to the list of potential suspects. Her lack of sleep since Tuesday was getting to her. She'd watched the video of Ariel's abduction so many times it replayed in her mind when she closed her eyes.

There was nothing remotely familiar about the masked man. Granted, he was only in the frame for a few seconds, but she was very much afraid the guy was a stranger to her and her family.

Yet the kidnapper would have had to see Lucy in person at some point. Her daughter was too young to have social media, and Lauren did not post any personal photos of herself and Lucy online. Obviously, Lauren's picture was posted all over the society pages, along with the charity websites for those she sponsored. But none of them included her daughter. That was one rule she didn't bend for anyone.

That meant this guy had been somewhere close by. Either here in the building where they lived or at the school. She'd asked for and received a list of all the school employees, but none of them had a criminal record. She'd asked the police to verify all the male school employees' alibis, but so far, they'd come up with nothing remotely suspicious.

Her father had provided a list of building employees, too, but those were still being vetted. She figured the police had abandoned that search once they'd gotten this Jorge Dombach in custody. That thought had her quickly scanning the employee list for his name.

It wasn't on either list. Based on the gunfire incident, she didn't believe Jorge was the man they were looking for so she didn't bother to add his name.

The names on her list blurred, and she pressed her fingertips to her eyes, trying to ward off a wave of exhaustion. She'd thought having Grady there would help her feel safe. Oh, she trusted Grady's expertise, but she still couldn't relax.

Just imagining Lucy going through the same experience she had was enough to make her blood run cold. She could not let this man get anywhere near her daughter.

Pushing away from her desk, Lauren changed into a pair of yoga pants and an oversized sweatshirt. If she had her way, she'd wear comfortable clothes every day, but her father expected her to look professional at all times. Rather funny now to think she'd worn an expensive pantsuit to meet Grady who had arrived in jeans and a black leather jacket.

She washed her face, ignoring the dark circles under her eyes. Maybe Grady had a point about canceling her charity events. Not the event itself, but making up an excuse as to why she couldn't attend.

It was a decision she didn't have to make now, so she turned and flipped the lights off on her way to bed. She'd barely crawled under the covers when she heard Lucy crying.

In a heartbeat, she was up and inside her daughter's room. "Shh, Lucy. It's okay. You're safe."

Her daughter lifted her tearstained face to look at her, then threw herself into her arms. "The masked man tried to get me," she sobbed.

"It's just a dream. He's not here. Grady is guarding us, remember?" She pressed a kiss to Lucy's temple. "You're safe, sweetie. I'm here and so is Grady."

Lucy's crying turned into a few hiccups. Then the little girl swiped at her face. "I don't want to have bad dreams."

"I know you don't." Lauren continued holding Lucy close, wishing there was a way to spare her daughter from having nightmares. A noise in the hallway caught her attention, and she looked over to see Grady hovering in the doorway. His thick brown hair was tousled, but she didn't think he'd been sleeping any more than she had.

He arched a brow, silently asking if everything was okay. She was touched by his concern. Granted, he was being paid to be there, but he seemed to care about Lucy. One thing was clear, he wasn't overly impressed with her wealth.

She smiled wearily and bobbed her head to let him know they were fine. He nodded and stepped back from the doorway to leave them alone. She had to squelch the urge to call him back.

Grady was a nice man. Different from what she'd expected, which was a good thing. She knew he would have rushed in to comfort Lucy if she hadn't gotten there first.

She wondered briefly why he was still single, then forced herself to concentrate on Lucy. Grady's lack of female companionship wasn't any of her business. The only reason she'd even asked about it was because she'd hoped to use the fake engagement ruse to her advantage. Obviously, their pretend engagement would only hold off the annoying men determined to pursue her for a short while. Once the kidnapper was caught, she and Grady would end their relationship. She could probably use her broken heart as an excuse to continue avoiding unwanted advances for a few weeks after that.

Maybe. At least for those who had half a brain.

Why didn't these men understand their attempt to pursue her was so exhausting? She had tried being polite, but many of them didn't know how to take no for an answer. Now she didn't bother to be nice, but even her rude and abrupt comments didn't seem to deter them.

Could one of them be involved in the kidnapping

attempt? A chill snaked down her spine at the thought. Maybe one of the men who were more persistent had arranged the kidnapping so he could heroically swoop in to save the child.

No, that was something out of a movie. Real life didn't work that way. She told herself to stop letting her imagination run wild. She couldn't believe any man who wanted to date her, with the goal of marrying her, would stoop that low.

This was the work of a stranger looking for easy cash or someone else who thought she owed them. Nelson would fit the bill perfectly, except for his being in jail. He could have arranged for someone else to do the dirty work, but how would her ex get access to the ransom demand? The more she considered that angle, the more that didn't play out for her either.

She was driving herself crazy imagining different scenarios. She gave herself a mental shake and continued to rock back and forth with her daughter cradled in her arms. When the little girl finally relaxed, she eased her down onto the bed and pulled up the covers.

"Stay with me," Lucy said sleepily.

"I will, sweetie. Go to sleep now." She stretched out beside her, listening as Lucy's breaths deepened. Lauren closed her eyes and tried to do the same. They were safe, now that Grady was nearby, watching over them. For the first time in what seemed like eons, rather than days, she relaxed.

She must have fallen asleep because something caused her to wake up. Pushing up on one elbow, she blinked in the darkness, looking down to make sure Lucy was still sleeping. Had she heard something? Or was it nothing more than her imagination?

Listening intently, she forced herself to relax. Maybe she'd heard Grady moving around. She'd left the door to Lucy's room open. She rolled away from Lucy to slip out of the bed. Her daughter hadn't moved, so she tiptoed past her to head to the door.

A loud *crack* followed by shattering glass startled her. She froze, trying to assimilate what she'd heard. It almost sounded like the gunfire that had shattered the back window of Grady's Jeep.

Then Grady was suddenly there. "Get your shoes and your coats while I grab Lucy." Without waiting for her to respond, he brushed past her to pick Lucy up from the bed, bringing her blanket along with the little girl. "We need to get out of here."

"What happened?"

"Hurry!" he snapped, carrying Lucy out of the room.

She darted into her bedroom to slide her feet into running shoes. Her heart thundered against her sternum as she followed Grady out to the living room. The cold wind blowing through the shattered window made her gasp in horror.

Someone had shot at the apartment!

"Move it," Grady said. "We can't stay here."

She gave a jerky nod, then grabbed her coat and Lucy's, belatedly realizing Grady was already wearing his.

"Do you have keys for the Porsche?" He had opened the door leading to the elevator vestibule and was staring out into the hallway.

"What's going on?" Lucy asked, her voice thick with sleep.

"Nothing to worry about, we're just going for a ride." Grady stepped forward and pushed the button to summon the elevator.

Lauren had to detour into the kitchen to grab the keys to the car. By the time she joined Grady, the elevator had arrived. She quickly entered the elevator, then used the keycard so the elevator would go all the way down to the parking garage.

"You need to take Lucy." He pushed the little girl into her arms, then pulled his gun from its holster, positioning himself in front of the doors. "I need my hands free in case . . ." He didn't finish, likely because Lucy was listening.

But she knew what he meant. He wanted his hands free in case there was another gunman waiting for them in the parking garage.

4

———

Grady swallowed the urge to curse, knowing he shouldn't have let his guard down even for a second. He'd stretched out on the sofa for what he called a combat nap. The sound of glass shattering beneath the force of the bullet had completely taken him by surprise. It burned to know he had not anticipated the threat would come through the floor-to-ceiling windows behind him, rather than the front door.

The elevator ride down to the parking garage seemed to take forever. It was a straight shot down from the thirty-sixth floor to the underground parking, but it still didn't move as quickly as he wanted. When the car finally stopped, he drew in a deep breath and edged a bit to the side, still making sure his body covered Lauren and Lucy. The doors slowly opened, and he waited. When nothing happened, he stepped out with his gun raised, sweeping the immediate area for a threat.

So far, so good. He glanced back at Lauren. "I'll drive. Please get Lucy in the car."

Lauren looked scared to death but did as he'd directed

without complaint. He continued sweeping his weapon across the area, noticing several new cars were parked in the garage since they'd last been down there. The video he'd taken wouldn't help him now, so he didn't bother to retrieve his phone. Instead, he waited until he heard the door of the Porsche slam before he quickly rounded the car and slid in behind the wheel.

He'd never driven a Porsche before, but he didn't let that stop him. He backed out of the parking spot, then cranked the wheel to drive toward the security gate. Thankfully, the gate lifted automatically, so he didn't have to stop.

"Where are we going?" Lauren asked as soon as he cleared the parking garage. He didn't immediately answer, distracted by a flash of headlights barreling toward them.

"Hold on!" Stomping on the gas, he wrenched the wheel again to turn left to avoid being hit. Lauren gasped but didn't scream as the car flew behind them, missing the Porsche by inches. He kept his foot down, weaving between other cars on the road to escape. The headlights were too bright for him to make out the make and model of the car that had nearly rammed into them, but he grimly realized the shooting at the penthouse apartment had been done for the sole purpose of flushing them out of the building.

A ruse that had pretty much worked. The only reason they were still alive was because Lauren's Porsche had a turbocharged engine under the hood, enabling him to escape the planned collision. The small size of the car had worked to their advantage too.

Yet the fancy, expensive sports car was more noticeable than he liked, which did not help their cause. He drove like a man on a mission, doing everything possible to avoid being followed.

When it was clear they'd gotten away, he murmured a

quick prayer of gratitude. Lauren shot him a questioning look but didn't say anything. He had learned about faith from the Sullivan family, although he didn't attend church as often as he knew he should. His schedule made that difficult. He hoped God didn't mind.

Traffic was lighter at three thirty in the morning, so he was able to zip through the city streets without too much difficulty, taking several turns to help throw off any possible tail. After a few moments, Lauren broke the silence. "I can give you directions if you tell me where we're going."

"We need to get out of the city." He glanced at her briefly, admiring her calm demeanor, then focused again on the road. "I'm open to suggestions."

"We spent a few summer vacations in Big Cedar Lake down in Missouri," she said. "It's a long drive, though, roughly nine hours from Chicago."

He shook his head. "That's no good if you've been there before. We need to head somewhere these guys wouldn't expect us to go."

She shot him an exasperated look. "I've never been to Ohio or Wisconsin. Does that help?"

"Yeah, it does." He quickly turned at the next intersection. "Let's find the interstate so we can head north to Wisconsin."

"Okay, keep going on this road for another couple miles." Lauren turned in her seat to look at her daughter. "Are you okay, Lucy?"

"Why is this happening?" Lucy's voice was small and frightened. His heart ached for the little girl. She didn't deserve this. And neither did Lauren.

"I don't know, sweetie. Some people choose to be mean and break the law." Lauren reached back to pat Lucy's knee.

"But Grady is going to keep us safe. Are you warm enough under the blanket?"

"Yeah." Lucy sniffed and wiped at her face. Grady belatedly realized that the little girl had been crying. She was in her booster seat, with the bedding wrapped around her. Her navy-blue parka was on the seat beside her. "Except for my toes."

"Here, let's wrap them up." Lauren unbuckled her seat belt so she could stretch back to use the end of the blanket to protect Lucy's feet. "Better?"

Lucy nodded. "Thanks."

Lauren's expression was somber as she settled back in her seat and reclasped her seatbelt. Grady wanted to say something reassuring, but he was all too aware that he'd almost gotten them killed.

Again.

Once they were on the interstate, he kept their speed within five miles of the posted limit. Despite his desire to get as far away from Chicago as humanly possible, he didn't want to be stopped by the local police.

Expensive cars like this Porsche were often targeted by law enforcement.

Silence stretched for several long minutes, then Lauren gestured to a building off to the side of the road. "My father has a plane hangar over there."

He barely glanced toward the dwelling. "I don't think using your father's plane is going to help. It's bad enough we're in your car." He glanced at the rearview, noticing Lucy was still awake and listening. "We'll switch this car out for something else when it's daylight. For now, I'm hoping the trip to Wisconsin throws them off."

"I understand." She turned to look at Lucy. "Try to get some sleep, sweetie, okay?"

"'Kay." Lucy yawned and rested her head back against the seat cushion. The plush leather seats were very comfortable, but he didn't think the booster seat was conducive to resting.

He kept his eye on the traffic behind them. The darkness along with the bright headlights made it impossible to identify specific vehicles by make or model. He debated getting off the interstate to use lesser-known highways, but he wasn't familiar with the area. Better to stay on the interstate for now, until they crossed the Illinois-Wisconsin border.

"She's going to need clothes and shoes," Lauren whispered.

"I know." He offered a reassuring smile, glancing at Lucy to see she appeared to be asleep. Keeping his voice soft, he added, "We'll find a place to shop once the stores open."

"I can't believe someone shot at the penthouse." Lauren shivered. He cranked the heat but knew the temperature wasn't the problem. It was the fear of how they were nearly caught. The crash had been designed to disable the vehicle long enough for the bad guys to grab Lucy. Or Lauren.

Maybe both.

"I think the car that tried to ram us was an SUV," Lauren murmured. "I only got a quick glance, though. It was dark in color—I can't say for sure it was black—and had tinted windows."

He arched a brow. "Good job. You saw more than I did."

A wry smile tugged the corner of her mouth. "You were busy pretending to be a race car driver."

That was true enough. His only goal had been to get Lauren and Lucy away unscathed. One thing about this recent turn of events bothered him, though. "There has to be more than one kidnapper involved."

"What do you mean?" Lauren frowned, then slowly

nodded. "The shooter and the driver of the SUV. There wasn't enough time between the two events to have been done by the same person."

"Exactly." He cut a quick glance to the rearview mirror. So far, he was reassured that most of the cars coming up from behind were passing them. Another good reason to stay within the posted speed limit. "We only saw the one masked man in the video, but he likely had someone driving the getaway car."

She frowned. "I don't remember the police mentioning two men. Only one."

"Maybe they decided to keep that bit of info to themselves. Or maybe Ariel was too scared to have noticed the driver." There were several factors that could have come into play. "But now we know for sure there are two men."

"We need to call Detective Kramer and Lieutenant Olson. I'm also worried about what Clara might find when she arrives in a few hours."

"The bad guys will be long gone by then. Hopefully, Clara will call the police." He glanced at Lauren. "I'm sorry she'll walk into a mess, but my only goal was to get you and Lucy to safety."

"I understand." She grimaced. "I just hope Clara can forgive me."

He nodded in understanding. He felt bad, but he was convinced Clara would be fine.

"I forgot my phone." Lauren patted her coat pockets. "I don't even have any cash."

He had some cash that Rex had given him. Emergency funds, which he realized was exactly what they'd landed in the middle of. An emergency. Besides, he could get additional cash through Rex if needed. "Don't worry about it. I'm glad you don't have your phone." He lowered his window and tossed his out. "It's more important that we stay off-grid."

"But—" Lauren cut herself off and sighed. "Never mind. You're right. I've never been in a position like this before. It's a little surreal to be honest."

"We'll be fine." He mentally added replacement phones to the list of things they needed to buy. "Try to get some rest. I'll let you know when I find a place to stay."

She glanced at him, then slid down in the seat. "Thank you, Grady."

He winced, knowing she shouldn't be thanking him. It was only due to God's grace that they'd escaped.

Certainly not his dubious expertise.

Grady continued driving, somewhat relieved when they were off the toll road and had crossed into Wisconsin. Toll readers recorded license plates. How much time did they have before the kidnappers found them?

Between getting rid of the Porsche, finding a place to stay, and obtaining additional funds over and above what he had in his pocket, Grady knew they were still living on borrowed time.

And the most frustrating part of all was that they were no closer to figuring out who might be behind these kidnapping attempts.

Attempts that had escalated in an alarming manner. Was this still about easy cash? Or something closer to revenge?

Grady could only pray the police would find out something very soon. Before it was too late.

Lauren dozed intermittently, her whirling thoughts keeping her from falling asleep. She'd been surprised by

Grady's whispered prayer and wondered if he always leaned on his faith while he was in danger. Maybe she should try praying more often. The hospital chapel had been her saving grace during Lucy's illness.

The terrain around them was peacefully beautiful. Not as breathtaking as the view of Lake Michigan, but the evergreen trees with their snow-tipped branches were pretty and seemed to absorb the traffic noise. Wisconsin was much quieter in general compared to downtown Chicago.

Then again, she assumed Cody, Wyoming, was even more quiet.

When Grady pulled into a gas station, she straightened in her seat. The lights were bright enough that she had to lift her hand to shield her eyes.

"Stay here, I'm just filling the tank." Grady's soft voice broke the silence.

"Since we're here, we should use the restroom." She unbuckled her seat belt. "I'm surprised Lucy made it this long."

He nodded. "Okay, it makes sense to use the facilities while we have the chance. I'll escort you both inside."

She wasn't about to argue, although she felt certain the danger was over. At least, for now. She slid out of the car and then moved the seat forward to reach into the back. "Lucy? We're going to use the bathroom, okay?"

Lucy blinked and stared up at her. Then she frowned. "I don't have my shoes."

"I know, I'll carry you." Lauren moved the blanket, then helped Lucy get her coat on over the pajamas. When she reached in to lift Lucy into her arms, Grady nudged her aside.

"I'll carry her." He effortlessly lifted the girl into his arms and carried her inside the gas station. She followed, blinking as her eyes slowly becoming accustomed to the bright interior lights.

The place was more than a gas station, it was a convenience store too. The scent of coffee was strong. There were baked goods and even some items of clothing, although nothing for a seven-year-old girl. Strangely, there were some socks, though, and she snagged a pair as they walked past. They would be too large for Lucy, but they were better than nothing.

Grady set Lucy down, then nodded at the socks. "Good idea. I'll grab us some coffee too. Are you hungry?"

"Having something to eat would be good." She smiled, then urged Lucy into the bathroom. Five minutes later, they emerged to find Grady standing near the food case. She eyed the hard-boiled eggs and yogurt, ignoring how Grady had grabbed a giant blueberry muffin.

"Can I have a donut?" Lucy looked excited at the prospect.

"Yes, but you need to eat something besides that." She found a children's brand of yogurt and grabbed another container of eggs. Then she hesitated, hoping Grady had enough cash on him to pay for everything. "Maybe I should use the ATM."

"Nope. We're not leaving an electronic trail. I've got this." He carried their items to the counter, along with two cups of coffee and a small container of milk for Lucy. She watched nervously as the clerk rang up their bill. She didn't normally worry about how much things cost and was surprised at the large total.

"That's crazy expensive," she whispered as Grady picked Lucy back up into his arms to carry her outside. "It's not even that much food."

He shrugged, offering a wry smile. "Says the woman

who probably hasn't stopped at a gas station ever in her life."

That was true, so it was hard to argue. She normally asked one of the security guards to fill her car up for her, when she even bothered to drive herself from point A to point B. It was strange to buy things with cash rather than using her credit card.

But she was still horrified at how much money Grady was spending out of his own pocket. Then again, she'd paid Grayson's Guardians the going rate including expenses. Grady would likely be reimbursed.

Dawn peeked over the horizon. As she opened their food purchases for Lucy, Grady filled the gas tank. Lucy drank her milk and ate her donut first, dropping crumbs in the back seat. Not that Lauren cared about the mess. The large socks went all the way up to Lucy's knees, but they were thick and warm, which was all that mattered. Lucy was so preoccupied with her donut treat that she didn't complain.

When Grady finished paying for their gas, he slid in behind the wheel. "All set?"

"Yes." She opened his muffin and handed it to him. "I can't believe it's already almost six in the morning."

"Yeah. The clerk mentioned a series of outlet malls about two hours away. They don't open until nine, but they should have what we need." He took a bite of his muffin and then drove out of the gas station parking lot.

They ate and sipped coffee in silence for a few minutes. Lucy had finished her food and was resting again with her eyes closed. It was hard to tell if her daughter was really sleeping or just pretending.

"I wish I could call Clara." She glanced at Grady. "She's

worked for us for almost ten years. I feel bad not knowing if she's okay."

"We'll get phones at the outlet mall." He frowned, then added, "But I think you should call the police, not Clara directly. I don't know if these guys have the ability to track phone calls or not."

She grimaced. "Okay, that's fine."

"I've been thinking about following up with the FBI. Do you know if they're letting law enforcement take the lead on the case?"

"Yes." She hadn't liked the decision. "Like I said, after Ariel was released, they didn't seem to be acting with a strong sense of urgency."

"Well, they'd better get cracking now," Grady drawled. She found his western accent cute. "Because the danger sure hasn't gone away."

"I know. I think the agent I spoke to was David Braun."

"I know an FBI agent back in Wyoming too. I'll go through him first. See if he has any insight to add."

She frowned. "I can't imagine Wyoming has much experience in this sort of thing."

"You'd be surprised. There's crime everywhere, unfortunately."

"Mommy, is the masked man going to find us?" Lucy asked.

She swiveled in her seat to smile reassuringly at her daughter. "The masked man has no idea where we are. We're in Wisconsin, a completely different state from Illinois."

"Good." Lucy's gaze was solemn. "Because I don't want to be scared anymore."

Her stomach knotted at the revelation. She would have

given anything to spare her daughter from this horror. "I know, sweetie."

"We're going to stop to do some shopping," Grady chimed in. "Do you like to shop, Lucy?"

Lucy shook her head. "I don't go shopping. Clara brings me what I need."

Grady arched a brow at that but dropped the subject. Lauren forced a smile. "It will be fun. You can pick out whatever you like."

"Can I dress like Ariel?" Lucy asked.

"Ah, sure. If you can find something similar." Lauren hoped she wasn't setting the little girl up for failure. She had no idea where Ariel's mother purchased her daughter's clothes. Ariel's private school tuition was being subsidized by Lauren and other wealthy families who paid extra to include those who couldn't afford to attend without assistance.

"Okay." Lucy looked excited at the thought of finding something similar to what her best friend wore.

A best friend whose mother had cut off all communication after the kidnapping.

Swallowing a sigh, she turned and watched the passing scenery. With the sun brightening the horizon, her heart filled with hope about the day ahead. The awful events from the previous evening and early morning hours faded away. It was as if nothing bad could reach them here in the middle of nowhere. The beautiful surroundings reminded her of their vacations in Big Cedar Lake. Lots of trees and rolling hills. Miles between cities, with nothing but wilderness in between.

Was she doing a disservice keeping Lucy in the city? No, Lauren had grown up in the city and turned out fine. This was their life; they couldn't just go somewhere small and pretend they weren't wealthy. Besides, she traveled with Lucy to new and exciting places over holiday breaks from school.

Yet as she looked at the woods around them, she wondered if their next trip should be to someplace remote and peaceful like this.

They went through a couple of bigger cities along the way, hitting some congested traffic thanks to road construction. Still, the hours passed faster than she'd anticipated. When Grady indicated the outlet malls advertised at the next exit, she craned her neck to see what sorts of stores were featured. None of the brands were familiar, but that was okay. It wasn't like she was planning to buy anything fancy. Especially since she had no idea how much money Grady had left to spend.

She decided they'd focus on the basics for Lucy, nothing more. She could keep wearing her yoga pants and sweatshirt.

Grady pulled into an empty parking space but didn't kill the engine. He glanced at his watch and shrugged. "We still have a few minutes until they open."

She hesitated. "I think Lucy just needs jeans, a sweatshirt, shoes, and socks. Hopefully, they won't be too expensive."

"Sounds good." If he was worried about the prices of the items they needed, he didn't let on.

"And don't forget the replacement phones." She had noticed there was a department store across the street. "I need to follow up with the police."

"I won't." He nodded toward the store closest to them. "Looks like they're unlocking the doors now."

"Great." She pushed out of the passenger seat. As before, Grady insisted on carrying Lucy inside. The store had plenty of options, and Lucy ran straight to a rack of pink sweatshirts. "Ooh, I like this one."

She eyed the price tag, then realized that was silly since she didn't know how much money Grady had. She handed it to him. "You need to stop her when you've reached your limit."

"No worries. I'm good." He didn't even look at the price, simply setting the items on the counter. "Just get what you need. I'm going to head over to buy the phones and a few other things."

They continued to shop while he got what they needed. She found a pair of sneakers in Lucy's size, along with a pair of jeans and pink socks that matched the sweatshirt. It took a while to make sure the items would fit. Grady returned, carrying a large plastic bag. He came up to stand beside her as she was eyeing a pair of snow boots in Lucy's size. She didn't know where they'd end up and figured the boots might be necessary.

Grady reached over to grab the pair she'd been looking at, adding it to the pile on the counter. "Anything else?"

She flushed. "I think we're good."

Grady nodded and quickly paid the bill. Again, it seemed like a lot for a store that was allegedly offering discounted bargains. But she kept her thoughts to herself, even as she realized this was the sort of thing Ariel's mother probably wrestled with every day.

When they were finished with their purchases, she took Lucy into the dressing room to change into her new things. Lucy seemed excited to have the everyday clothes. She even insisted on wearing her new snow boots.

When they emerged from the dressing room, she caught Grady's grim gaze and instantly knew something was wrong. "What?"

"This way." He took the bag from her hands and led them quickly to a side exit. She didn't understand why he was so upset, until he glanced back through the clear glass of the front door.

That's when she saw it too. A black SUV with tinted windows was driving slowly past the store.

She sucked in a harsh breath. The kidnappers had found them!

5

———

Grady had expected the kidnappers would eventually find Lauren's Porsche, it wasn't exactly the kind of car that was useful in staying off-grid. But they'd gotten here far quicker than he'd anticipated. How had they known they'd come to Wisconsin? Was it as simple as accessing electronic toll information?

There wasn't time to worry about how the black SUV had found them there. He needed to get Lauren and Lucy out of harm's way. Ducking out the side door to the shopping mall, he thrust Lauren and Lucy behind him as he quickly scanned the parking lot. They needed a ride out of there and fast.

"Where are we going?" Lucy asked.

"Shh. We need to be quiet, okay?" Lauren's voice was a hushed whisper, as if she feared the kidnappers could hear her from the other side of the building. He hated knowing they were in danger.

Again.

It took a minute for him to spot their best option. After making his choice, he glanced over his shoulder at Lauren.

"Stay beside me as much as possible. We're heading for that dark blue car, third in from the corner."

Lauren frowned in confusion, clearly not understanding his intent. Yet she would soon enough. He took a step forward, subtly urging Lauren and Lucy to keep pace beside him. He strode quickly toward the vehicle in question. It was a later model car that was well known to be easy to hot-wire. By God's grace, he'd even purchased a USB drive along with a small laptop computer when he'd picked up the new phone.

The drive would come in handy now.

He was shocked to discover the car door wasn't locked. Maybe that was a Wisconsin thing, the way it was in Wyoming. Crime wasn't as rampant way out here away from the big city. Squashing a flash of guilt, he turned to Lauren and Lucy. "Get in."

Lauren glared at him. "Are you nuts? We can't steal a car."

"Get in." He glanced back over his shoulder, half expecting the black SUV to have made it around the building. "We don't have time to argue about this. We'll make things right later, okay?"

Her expression troubled, Lauren nodded and opened the back door for Lucy. He fished in the bag for the USB drive and then tossed the bag onto the floor of the back seat. He bent down and broke away the plastic casing around the steering column. It was easier than he'd expected, possibly because the cold temperatures made the plastic brittle. When he'd removed the casing, he could see how easy it was to insert the tip of the USB drive into the opening. Turning it, the engine roared to life.

No wonder so many of these types of cars had been stolen, he thought as he slid in behind the wheel. With Lucy in the back, Lauren quickly settled in beside him. He glanced at her as he backed out of the parking space. "You and Lucy need to keep your heads down until we're far away from here."

"Okay." Lauren's voice was subdued. She still didn't look happy about what he'd done. She turned in her seat. "Put your head down, Lucy, okay?"

"Okay." He could tell Lucy was scared, but she did as her mother asked. Grady headed toward a side exit, keeping an eye on the rearview mirror for either the owner of the car he'd stolen or the black SUV with tinted windows.

Once they were on the road, he headed west to avoid driving past the front of the shopping mall. After a few miles, he said, "Lauren, you and Lucy can sit up now."

"Thanks." She lifted her head, then turned to look at her daughter. "Are you okay, Lucy?"

"Yeah." Lucy frowned. "But why did we change cars?"

Lauren appeared at a loss for how to respond. Grady met Lucy's gaze in the rearview mirror. "I saw a suspicious car back at the mall and thought it was better for us to switch to a different vehicle, just in case."

"We're safe, Lucy." Lauren reached back to pat her daughter's knee. "Don't worry."

Lucy nodded and looked less scared, which was a good thing. Grady fell silent as he followed the winding highway lined with trees on either side of the road. Only after they'd traveled a solid ten miles from the shopping mall and the interstate did he relax his tense muscles.

Even then, he knew the danger was far from over. Maybe they'd escaped the kidnappers, but they were still in a stolen car. He was glad they'd gotten warm clothes and shoes for Lucy, along with the electronics he'd wanted.

Now they needed to find a place to stay.

As they approached an intersection, he decided to turn right, heading north. The farther they stayed away from civilization, the better.

"I'll pay the owner for the car," Lauren said in a low voice.

He nodded, not surprised by her comment. "I'm sure Rex can reimburse the owner too. I wouldn't have taken drastic action if I'd had another option."

"I understand." She tucked her blond hair behind her ear. "I had no idea it was so easy to . . ." She let her voice trail off, no doubt not wanting to say too much in front of Lucy.

"It's only this make and model; most vehicles had additional safeguards built in." He was glad she wasn't dwelling too much on what he'd done. "Keep your eyes open for a place to stay."

She nodded and glanced both ways. A frown furrowed her brow. "I don't see much of anything way out here."

"We'll find something sooner or later." He glanced at the gas tank and breathed a sigh of relief that they had three-quarters of a tank. Gas stations had cameras that could be used to track a stolen car.

"What did you buy at the electronics store?" Lauren bent over to look inside the bag. "A computer?"

"I figured we could do some investigating on our own." He didn't want to add the part that being alone with Lauren and Lucy for hours doing nothing would drive him nuts. "I know it's a long shot, but it can't hurt to do a little digging."

"And the USB drive?" She tapped the item in question that still sat in the ignition, much like a key.

He grimaced. "Honestly, I grabbed it at the last minute. I thought that we might need it to store a video or other images." He was vague on purpose, not wanting to mention his thought process in front of Lucy. The disposable phones could record a video, but he hadn't been sure of how much data they could store. The devices he'd purchased were relatively basic, without any of the bells and whistles of a smartphone.

As it turned out, the USB drive had been a lifesaver in a very different way.

"I see." Lauren's troubled expression indicated she didn't really follow his logic, but she dropped the issue.

If circumstances had been different, he'd have used their new phone to record the black SUV driving by, hoping to get a license plate. He hadn't noticed if the outdoor mall had cameras mounted on the exterior of the building. If they did, the police may be able to get that information.

The possibility of getting a lead on the kidnappers made him feel better. Keeping a wary eye on the speedometer, no point in speeding in a stolen car, he continued driving north. There wasn't much traffic on the rural highway. He hoped there wouldn't be many cops out either.

The first town they came across was Columbia. It had a few hotels, but he wanted something with more anonymity. Another fifteen miles later, they came upon the much smaller town of Fullerton.

"Look, Grady, there's a sign for cabin rentals." Lauren gestured to the billboard on the right. "It says it's six miles away, so I assume it's located farther outside of town."

"Perfect." The directions indicated they should go to the northeast. They were far enough from the shopping mall that he wasn't worried the black SUV could track them. When they came upon the cabin rentals, he slowed and turned into a plowed driveway leading to a main dwelling.

He put the gearshift into park but kept the engine running. "I'd like you and Lucy to stay here. I'll get us a cabin."

"Okay," Lauren agreed.

Pushing out of the car, he scanned the area. It was desolate and private, two solid points in their favor. He could see a couple of individual cabins off to the right. The billboard had boasted ten cabins, but he could only see five of them. Maybe the others were tucked farther away from the road. If so, those were the ones he was interested in.

He opened the door and stepped into the main lodge. There was nobody behind the front counter, but he noticed there were several racks displaying touristy stuff for sale. Stuffed bears, bobcats, and deer, along with jars of honey and jam, presumably homemade. He stepped up to the counter and rang the small bell. A woman in her mid-sixties came out to greet him.

"How can I help you?" she asked.

"I'm here with my wife and daughter. We'd like to stay in one of your cabins." He smiled reassuringly. "We'd like one deeper in the woods if possible. This is my wife's first trip to the area, and she's hoping to see some wildlife while we're here."

"Mostly deer in February," the woman said, eyeing him in a way that made him wonder if she was suspicious of his request. "You might see a bobcat, though, the female had cubs last year. They're about grown now."

"That's great." He injected enthusiasm into his tone as he pulled out his wallet. He was running low on cash, despite the fact that Rex had given him two grand to use for emergencies. He still needed to buy some food for the next day or two as well. "Thanks so much. I hope you don't mind if we pay in cash." He lowered his voice. "My wife maxed out our credit card, so I shredded it."

To his relief, the woman shrugged as if it didn't matter one way or the other. "Cash works for me."

Five minutes later, he was back in the stolen car. He handed Lauren one of the keys to cabin number 7. "We're set until tomorrow morning."

She arched a brow. "Just one night?"

"Yeah. For now." He drove around the main lodge to the cabins located behind it. They should be safe enough staying here for the rest of the day and through the night until morning. Since he still wasn't sure how the kidnappers had tracked them all the way to the outlet mall in Wisconsin, he didn't dare make long-term plans. Better to take things day by day.

While hoping and praying he could keep Lauren and Lucy safe until they understood the source of the threat.

LAUREN WAS HOLDING on to her composure by a thread. She'd never in her life broken the law, and she could barely comprehend that she'd participated in stealing a car! Granted, she'd gladly reimburse the owner, but for all she knew, they'd left the owner stranded inside one of the stores without any means of getting home. What if the owner had kids? What if taking the car meant the owner couldn't go to work?

The endless possibilities zipped around in her mind until she wanted to scream. But of course, she didn't. Instead, she opened the back door of the stolen car to let Lucy out as Grady headed up to unlock the cabin door.

Lauren hunched her shoulders at the chill in the room. Grady found the thermostat, cranked it up, then crossed the room to start a fire. The interior of the cabin was rustic but nice. Wooden floors were covered with colorful rugs, and the furniture was simple yet comfortable. There was a small kitchenette, and for the first time in hours, she belatedly realized she was hungry.

"We'll need to get some groceries." She crossed the room to peer into the two bedrooms. One held a queen-sized bed, and the other had two twin beds. Satisfied, she turned to head back into the main living area. They needed food for lunch, dinner, and breakfast the following morning. How much that would cost, she had no clue.

"I know. We'll head there next." Grady didn't appear concerned about their financial situation. "I just want to get our phones charged and ready to go. We'll make our calls when we're back in town."

She nodded, belatedly remembering her determination to call the local police back in Chicago. The shooting event from the middle of the night seemed like eons ago rather than hours. And what about Clara? Their long-term house-keeper didn't live in the penthouse with them, but that didn't mean she wasn't in danger. Someone could easily try to use force against Clara to obtain information about her daughter.

Just for easy money? Or was this about something else? But what? It didn't make any sense. There was absolutely no reason to go after Lucy other than to force her or her father to pay a ransom.

The only person who could be seeking revenge was her ex-husband, Nelson Derringer. He wouldn't have nearly enough money to pay someone to do this.

Unless the person involved had negotiated a portion of the ransom as payment.

She swallowed hard and turned her attention to Lucy. Her daughter was at the living room window, gazing out at the snowy landscape. Her daughter frowned, then shot

Lauren a look of reproach. "I thought we'd see wild animals here."

"The lady in charge said there's a bobcat family that lives in the woods nearby. But I don't think you'll see them until dusk. Or dawn," Grady said. "She also mentioned there are a lot of white-tailed deer in the area."

"Bobcats?" Lauren paled. "Are you sure it's safe here?"

"Yes, don't worry." He shot her an amused glance. "They won't bother us. They prey on small animals, not people."

Easy for him to say, she thought darkly. There hadn't been any bobcats at the Big Cedar Lake in Missouri. At least, not that she was aware of.

When Grady finished with the phones, he handed her one. "Do you know the number of the police station? If not, I can use the computer to find it."

"I don't have the number memorized, so please look it up for me." She felt foolish, but really, how many people in the world knew their local police department phone numbers by heart? Especially in this age of smartphones?

Less than a minute later, Grady had the number. She entered it into her phone but didn't put the call through. She knew he wanted her to wait until they were away from the cabin.

Grady pocketed his phone. "Ready to go?"

She nodded. "Lucy, let's decide what you want for lunch and dinner, okay?"

"How about pepperoni pizza?" Lucy and Grady both said at the exact same time.

She couldn't help but smile as her daughter dissolved into a fit of giggles. Lauren rolled her eyes and threw up her hands in surrender. "Captain Jack's pizza it is."

Lauren wondered how big of a risk they were taking by heading back into the town of Fullerton. She felt as if they were driving a car that had stolen written across the back window in neon paint. But surprisingly, they didn't pass a single police car on the road.

She wasn't sure that the lack of a police presence was a good thing. What if the bad guys showed up there? They could all be dead before anyone from law enforcement arrived.

Not dead, she grimly reminded herself. *Alive.* The goal was to take Lucy alive in order to make a ransom demand.

If that's what was going on here.

When they reached the city limits, Grady nodded at her. "Go ahead and make your call."

She pushed the send button on her phone and waited. A female voice asked how she should direct the call. "I'd like to speak to either Lieutenant Olson or Detective Kramer please. It's important."

"Hold please." A moment later, Lauren was annoyed to hear a recorded voice in her ear. *You've reached Lieutenant Olson. Please leave a message.*

"Lieutenant, this is Lauren Chandler. I'm calling about the shooting at my penthouse apartment earlier this morning. Please call me back right away." She ended the call without giving her phone number because she had no idea what it was. "That was useless," she told Grady. "I don't even know my own phone number."

"I'm sure they have caller ID. He'll call you back." Grady smiled reassuringly.

"Yeah, okay." She tried to shake off her frustration. Maybe the lieutenant was still at her penthouse apartment, checking out the scene of the crime. She stared down at the cheap disposable phone for a moment, then tucked it into the pocket of her winter coat.

Grady pulled into the parking lot of a grocery store. He

backed into a space that was at the far end of the building, well away from any other cars. She was about to ask why when she realized the USB drive was still being used as a car key.

Yeah, this was a big risk. She glanced back at Lucy, then at Grady. "Maybe we should wait here."

"Too cold and we're low on gas." He glanced around, then killed the engine. "Let's just make this quick, okay?"

She nodded and pushed out of the car. Lucy did the same, skipping alongside them as they headed inside.

"Sandwiches for lunch and eggs and toast for breakfast?" Grady asked the questions as he made his way to the bread aisle. "We need to keep things simple."

"That's fine." There was no point in worrying about eating healthy at this point. "Coffee, too, please."

He flashed a grin. "That goes without saying."

She smiled back, thinking that under different circumstances, this would be fun. Grady wasn't like any man she'd ever known. Certainly not like those who chased her at various charity events. He was calm and cool in a crisis, having gotten them to safety several times now since this nightmare started. He always seemed to have everything under control.

She was deeply grateful he'd been the one assigned to her case.

He paid for their groceries, then ushered them back to the stolen car. He set the bags on the floor of the back seat, started the car, then pulled away from the store.

As they were heading back to the highway, she caught a glimpse of a black-and-white squad car. She reached over to grab Grady's arm. "Do you see him?"

"Yeah." Grady's jaw was tight. "Don't stare over there. I'm going to turn at the next intersection."

"Okay." She didn't let go of his arm as he made the turn. She braced herself for the cop to flip on his red and blue lights and come racing after them.

He didn't. But it was a close call that frayed her temper.

"We need a different car," she hissed.

"I know, but it's not like a town this size has a rental car facility that we can use, even if I can get Rex to make the arrangements." He glanced at her. "We're okay for a little while. The cabin we're staying in is well off the main roads."

She forced herself to release her death grip on his arm. "Fine. But please get in touch with Rex Grayson, sooner rather than later."

"That's the plan." Grady remained focused on driving. It took her a minute to realize they were in a neighborhood where small houses lined both sides of the street. The area looked as if they could have been in a middle-income Chicago suburb rather than in a different state entirely.

By the time Grady made his way through the area to the highway, she managed to relax. Before she could say anything, her phone buzzed with an unfamiliar ringtone.

Eyeing the display, she recognized the number she'd used to call the Chicago PD. "Hello?"

"Is this Lauren Chandler?" a deep voice demanded. She thought it was Lieutenant Olson, but she wasn't sure.

"Who is this?" she asked, instead of answering in the affirmative.

"Detective Kramer. Olson told me you called him about the shooting at your penthouse last night." The detective sounded annoyed. "Where are you? I need you and Grady to give me a statement about what happened here."

"We're safe, thanks to Grady." She glanced at Grady, knowing he was listening to her side of the conversation. As was her daughter. "Are you still at the penthouse now? Is

Clara, my housekeeper, there? I'd like to know she's unharmed."

"She was here, but we sent her home." Kramer's tone had calmed down a bit. "She was the one who called us. Said the place was empty when she arrived early this morning and that the window was shattered."

Lauren closed her eyes, grateful to know Clara was unharmed. Probably scared, but otherwise fine. She thought of how Grady prayed and sent up a silent prayer for God to keep Clara safe. "Thank you for letting me know. Unfortunately, there isn't much I can tell you. The window shattered, so Grady got us out of there."

"Looks like somebody shot the window," Kramer said. "We found a slug in the drywall across from the window."

A slug. How close had Grady come to being hit? She shivered and tried to remain calm. "Yes, that's what happened. We left via the parking garage, but there was a car waiting for us there. The driver drove straight toward us, trying to cause a crash, but Grady was able to avoid being hit."

"Where was this?" Kramer asked. "Did either of you get a good look at the car?"

"No, it was too dark, and I think the driver had his high-beam lights on. They were very bright." She thought back to those harrowing moments when they'd nearly been hit. "All we can say for sure is that the car was dark in color."

She was about to go into detail about the black SUV with tinted windows that showed up outside the outlet mall when Kramer spoke again. "Well, the good news is that we have a new lead to follow up on."

"What new lead?" She glanced at Grady who had turned into another neighborhood of homes. These were a little nicer and bigger than the others they'd passed. Clearly, he didn't want to go back to the cabin until she'd finished the call.

"Does the name Joe O'Neil sound familiar?" Kramer asked.

She frowned, then nodded, even though she knew Kramer couldn't see her. "Yes, Joe O'Neil was a security guard that worked for my father. He left our employment maybe nine months ago? I don't understand. Why are you looking at him?"

"Do you know why he left your father's employment?" Kramer pressed.

"No, I assumed he got another job." Even as she said the words, she realized that wasn't likely. Most of the staff at the Savion building enjoyed their work, and she knew they were paid a decent salary. Better than most of the other security guard positions.

"We were told by your building manager, Mark Jonas, that O'Neil was fired for theft."

The news shocked her. "What did he steal?"

"He stole items from some of the residents' apartments. Not yours, that would have been too obvious," Kramer added. "From what I understand, they didn't figure out it was him right away because he was able to tamper with the security video to mask his movements. And he chose apartments that were undergoing remodeling. When he was arrested, he had stolen jewelry from Mrs. Ashley Pauly's apartment. He returned those items but still did a few months in jail."

She couldn't believe it. Why hadn't anyone mentioned the details about O'Neil's arrest to her? "And you think Joe O'Neil has decided to try another way to get money?"

"Yep. We have issued a BOLO for him. Where are you?" Kramer sounded cranky again. "We still need to talk."

"I'll be in touch. Thanks for letting me know." She quickly ended the call and shut down the phone.

Was Kramer right about the former security guard? Had Joe O'Neil really decided to try to kidnap Lucy to get a big payday? She wanted to think it would be that easy.

But she couldn't bring herself to believe it.

6

—————

"What was that about a man named O'Neil?" Grady glanced at Lauren as he pulled away from the curb.

"My father's manager fired him for theft nine months ago." She shook her head, looking dazed. "Detective Kramer has issued a BOLO, whatever that means, for him."

"The acronym stands for 'be on the lookout,'" Grady explained. "But it's a stretch to think this guy would go from stealing stuff to kidnapping." Not to mention shooting at them, but he didn't add that because Lucy was in the back listening. "Does he have any police or military background that you're aware of?"

"No." She glanced at him, then back at Lucy and nodded. "You're wondering about the penthouse window."

"Yep." He wasn't sure anyone who lived and worked in the city made time to shoot weapons at a firing range. Unless that person happened to be an avid hunter. Most of the men and women in Wyoming could hit what they were aiming at, but they lived in small towns nestled near forests and mountains. Not skyscrapers. "Seems a stretch to me."

"I agree." Lauren frowned. "He would also know what Lucy looks like. I can't imagine he'd kidnap another child by mistake."

He shrugged and made his way back to the highway that would take them to their cabin rental. "Some people aren't as observant as others, but I really don't think he's our guy."

"Yeah." She sighed. "I was hoping he was, though."

He understood her concern. She wanted this kidnapper/shooter caught and thrown behind bars. He wanted that too. But he wasn't going to let his guard down either. The black SUV with tinted windows was fresh in his mind. They'd escaped, but he still didn't understand how the driver of the car found them in the first place.

He made a mental note to discuss options with FBI Special Agent Griffin Flannery. Griff was married to Alexis Sullivan and lived on the Sullivan K9 Search and Rescue Ranch with the other Sullivan siblings. The property was forty minutes southeast of Cody. Grady had met the guy a few times, mostly after Joel or Justin Sullivan caused damage to his house while they borrowed the place to escape from danger. He hadn't really minded that they made themselves at home. They were good people who had followed through on paying for the repairs. He and the twins, Joel and Justin, had gone to school together. He'd enjoyed the times he'd stayed at the Sullivan ranch.

Grady knew he could trust Griff to be straight with him. The black SUV should not have been able to find them at the strip mall in Wisconsin. Unless he'd overreacted and the car showing up had been a coincidence? No, he didn't think so. It was too similar to the one he'd seen the previous day. Deep down, he was beginning to suspect there might be a dirty cop involved in this scheme. And if that was the case, this was way more than a simple kidnapping for ransom.

Keeping a wary eye out for another cop, he left the city of Fullerton. He'd grabbed some black electrical tape from the grocery store so he could alter the license plate. The trick should buy them a little time, although in the daylight, it might be easy to spot the alteration.

The rest of the trip to the cabin was uneventful. He breathed a sigh of relief as he pulled up to cabin number 7. They were almost directly behind the main lodge, so the car and their cabin could not be seen from the main road.

"Let's help with the groceries, Lucy." Lauren pushed out of the car.

"I've got them." He quickly grabbed the five bags in two hands. "Just hold the door for me, okay?"

Lucy did so, and he belatedly realized Lauren had wanted her daughter to assist in the minor chore.

"Lucy, will you help put the groceries away?" He set the bags on the sturdy oak kitchen table.

"Okay." Lucy scrambled up on a chair so she could remove items from the bag. When Lauren sent him a grateful look, he nodded at her.

"I'm new to this," he murmured in a low voice.

"I know." She stored the frozen Captain Jack's pizzas in the freezer. "But I want her to be self-sufficient someday."

He understood but didn't mention that having Clara running the household wasn't likely to assist her in reaching that goal. It wasn't any of his business how Lauren raised her daughter. He was only there to pretend to be her fiancé and to keep them both safe from harm.

When the groceries had been put away, Grady set up the new computer and connected to the cabin rental Wi-Fi network. First, he entered Joe O'Neil's name into the search engine. There proved to be way too many possibilities, as Joe, Joseph, and Joey were all very common names. He considered calling Detective Kramer to get a date of birth for the guy but decided to wait until after he talked to Griff.

He did another search on Lauren's ex-husband, Nelson Derringer. The newspaper article related to Nelson's fatal car crash and his DUI arrest popped up on the screen. He scanned the information, a little disappointed there was nothing new to learn. The article did mention his friend Robert Morton who had been declared DOA at the hospital following the crash.

Nice to know that Nelson had been held responsible for his actions, he thought as he looked at the image of Robert Morton's smiling face. Drinking while driving was never good, and it always seemed to him that innocent people were more likely to die than the intoxicated driver.

There was no mention of Robert's blood alcohol level. He glanced at Lauren who was making sandwiches with Lucy for lunch. It was early, but their gas station breakfast had been hours ago.

"Do you know if Bobby was drinking at the time of the crash?"

Lauren nodded. "He and Nelson were both intoxicated. Nelson supposedly had less to drink than Bobby, but probably not by much. I feel bad that Bobby was killed, although they made the decision to go out drinking without a plan to get home safely."

"Yeah, in this day and age of rideshares and taxis, there's no excuse for that."

"Don't forget our subways," Lauren added. "That's why the judge threw the book at Nelson."

He did tend to forget about their mass transit system. There were no subways in Wyoming. "That too. It makes no sense to me that they wouldn't have used some other method to get home."

Lauren glanced at Lucy, then shrugged. "Nelson was arrogant. He thought he was better than everyone else."

He arched a brow. "I'm willing to bet that attitude hasn't lasted for long during his stint in jail."

Lauren smiled. "I think about that a lot. For his sake, I hope he comes out a better man."

He wanted to ask why she married him in the first place but let the subject drop. For one thing, her decision to date and marry Nelson wasn't relevant to the case. And for another, she clearly realized she'd made a mistake by ending it. For her sake and Lucy's, he was glad about that.

There was no reason to dwell on Lauren's personal life. It wasn't as if he was interested in making their engagement real. Aside of the fact that he had no desire to live in Chicago, he couldn't imagine Lauren putting up with his travel schedule. His previous girlfriend Becca hadn't lasted six months before moving on with someone else.

Enough. He gave himself a mental shake and turned his attention back to the computer. He did a search on Robert Morton, hoping to find more information, but again, the first name of Robert was fairly common. The computer search pulled up Robert Mortons from all across the United States.

"I'm calling Griff," he said, rising to his feet.

"Who?" Lauren frowned.

"Griffin Flannery, he's an FBI agent from Wyoming." He lifted a hand when she started to speak. "I know he probably doesn't know much about the FBI agents from Chicago, I just want to talk to him."

"Okay, lunch will be ready soon."

He stepped into the living room to make the call. He had to think for a moment about the number. He knew the Sullivans memorized each other's phone numbers for situations just like this. After a moment, he heard Griff's voice on the other end of the line. "Hello?"

"Griff, it's Grady McFarland. Do you have a few minutes to talk?"

"Absolutely. What's going on? I don't think anyone has damaged your house since before Christmas."

"I wouldn't know, I'm doing a job in Chicago, but am currently in the small town of Fullerton, Wisconsin."

"That's interesting. What do you need from me?"

He was impressed Griff didn't push for details. He quickly filled Griff in on the kidnapping attempt of Ariel Turner, then the multiple shootings that had sent them out of state. "Our problem now is that I'm not sure who we can trust. How easy is it to track a car through the tollway system? It's the only way I can think of that anyone could have found our location so quickly."

"The tollway system is accessible by law enforcement, not private citizens. Although having worked now for the past two months with Kendra's new husband, Dominic, I'm sure a hacker could get in easily enough," Griff said. "That doesn't fit the profile of your typical kidnapper."

"Yeah, I agree, they don't typically shoot at penthouse windows and cars either." Grady paused, then added, "I need help tracking a few names."

"I can do that." When Grady gave him the names of their current suspect, Joe O'Neil along with the names of Nelson and Bobby to expand on his ability to search for additional family members, Griff spelled them out to make sure he had them correct. "Do you also want me to touch base with the FBI in Chicago?"

"That would be great." Grady searched his memory for a moment. "I believe Lauren spoke to a David Braun. We've also been in contact with Detective Kramer and a Lieutenant Olson from the Chicago PD. Nobody knows we're in Fullerton, though. So don't let that information out."

"I'll keep your location confidential," Griff promised. "And let me see what I can do with these names. Are they all from Chicago?"

"As far as I know, yes. Nelson and Bobby were in a fraternity together at Loyola University."

"That will help me narrow it down." Griff sounded thoughtful. "Anything else I can do?"

"When you reach out to the FBI agent from Chicago, ask if he's been kept informed of the recent shooting attempts against Lauren and Lucy. I want to be sure the local police are doing their part in this."

"Not a problem," Griff said. "If this David Braun wants to talk to you and Lauren, can I give him this number?"

"Yes, that works. And thanks, Griff. I owe you one."

"Nope, you've helped the Sullivans over the past year when they were in trouble. This is the least I can do. I'll be in touch." With that, Griff ended the call.

Feeling better, Grady pocketed his phone and headed into the kitchen. Seeing the black electrical tape sitting on the counter, he remembered he needed to head outside to alter the license plates.

"Are you ready to eat?" Lauren set a plate of sandwiches to the table.

"Sure." He reached over to close the laptop, pushing it aside to make room. When Lauren and Lucy were both seated, he dropped into his chair, cleared his throat, and said, "I, um, would like to say grace."

Lauren flashed a startled glance at him, but then she nodded. "Of course. Lucy, fold your hands together like this." She demonstrated for her daughter.

"Why?" Lucy asked, doing what she was told.

"Because we're going to thank God for our blessings." He wasn't used to praying out loud, but having been around the Sullivans for years, he was no stranger to how it was done. "Dear Lord Jesus, we ask You to bless this food we are about to eat. We also ask that You keep us all safe in Your care as we seek the truth. Amen."

"Amen," Lauren echoed. She looked pointedly at Lucy until her daughter added, "Amen."

"There, now that we've said grace, we can dig into our meal." He grinned and took a big bite of his sandwich. He was glad Lauren and Lucy had participated in the prayer.

With the danger surrounding them, he knew they needed God's protection now more than ever.

LAUREN HAD ONLY HEARD part of Grady's side of the call with the Wyoming FBI agent. It was nice to know he had friends in law enforcement. She trusted Grady to keep her daughter safe.

And she wished, not for the first time, that Grady would stick around after the danger was over.

But that wasn't going to happen. Grady was clearly at home here in the middle of nowhere. Which was good because his skills were necessary to keep them hidden. But she couldn't imagine living in a place like this year-round.

"Can I play outside in the snow?" Lucy asked between bites of her sandwich. "I want to build a snowman."

"Oh, um, okay." She hadn't purchased snow pants for Lucy but had noticed there was a small washer and dryer unit tucked into the corner of the main bathroom.

"I can take her outside with me when I alter the license plate," Grady offered.

"Thanks." She'd have to head outside, too, she couldn't just leave Lucy out there alone, but she was grateful he'd be nearby as well. "I appreciate that."

When lunch was over, she asked Lucy to help with clearing the table. Deciding to wait to do dishes, she bundled Lucy up in her winter coat and new snow boots from the outlet mall.

Grady snagged the black electrical tape as he led the way outside. Lauren guided Lucy to the open area behind the cabin. Lucy enthusiastically dug her mittened hands into the snow, throwing it up into the air with glee. Watching the little girl made her chest tighten with love. That anyone would try to harm an innocent child made her angry.

"Come on, Mom, let's make a snowman!"

With a sigh, she did so. Grady worked on the license plate, then came over to help them. He worked faster than she did, expertly making a large ball of snow for the base.

By the time they'd finished, Lucy was shivering with cold. "Okay, let's go back inside now," Lauren said. "I need to dry your clothes."

"Yours too," Lucy said, eyeing her wet yoga pants.

"Yep." She was cold to the bone but hadn't wanted to stop Lucy from having fun. After everything they'd been through, they deserved some downtime.

"Your snowman looks great, Lucy." Grady grinned at her daughter.

"He needs a snow wife and kid," Lucy declared.

Lauren felt herself flush, knowing her daughter didn't mean that the way it sounded. "That's a project for another day. For now, let's go inside."

Inside the cabin, she took Lucy into the bedroom to have her strip out of her clothes. Then she wrapped the little girl in a blanket. "Have a seat on the sofa," she said, guiding her into the living room. "Maybe Grady can figure out how to work the television."

Grady nodded at her wet clothes. "I can do that, but you need to change too."

"I will. Do you have anything you want washed?" Again, her cheeks heated with embarrassment. When she'd asked for a bodyguard, she hadn't imagined they'd be living together in a log cabin in the middle of the woods.

"Why don't you let me wash the clothes?" He seemed to understand the source of her discomfort. "You sit on the sofa with Lucy. I'll take care of everything."

"You know how to do the laundry?" she asked in surprise.

"I've lived alone for years, so yeah, I know how to do the laundry." His dry western drawl made her smile.

Of course, Grady knew what to do. He seemed to be an expert on everything, from keeping her and Lucy safe to stealing a car and even mundane tasks like laundry.

As she stripped off her clothes and wrapped up in a blanket, she wondered if there was anything Grady couldn't do. And quickly decided there wasn't.

After he threw their wet clothes into the dryer, he found a children's station on the television, then sat at the table, also wrapped in a blanket from the waist down, to work on the computer. When she caught herself drifting to sleep, she straightened and made her way to the kitchen to join him.

"Can I help?" She leaned over to see the screen. She was surprised to see Nelson's mug shot. "Wow, he really looks awful."

Grady nodded. "He was probably coming to grips with knowing that life as he knew it was over."

She looked away, suddenly embarrassed. "I'm sure you're wondering why I married him in the first place."

Grady shrugged. "I'm sure he was on his best behavior."

She let out a harsh laugh. "That's an understatement. He was sweet, charming, and spent money on little gifts for me. I thought it was nice how he paid for everything while we were dating. He seemed indifferent to my trust fund. I'm ashamed to say I really bought into his act. A few months after the wedding, I discovered I was pregnant." She fell silent, lost in memories of the past. She'd been so excited to learn about her pregnancy.

"What happened?" Grady asked softly. He kept his voice low, the way she did, so Lucy couldn't overhear.

"Nelson seemed happy about the baby, but it didn't take long for our relationship to unravel. He started drinking more, buying expensive Scotch. He also spent more time with his old frat buddies, like Bobby Morton. But it wasn't until I overheard him talking to someone about how he was planning to invest a quarter of a million dollars into some new enterprise that things got nasty. I discovered Nelson was in debt after our marriage. He claimed it was investments that had gone south. So when I heard him making that deal, I knew he didn't have two hundred and fifty thousand dollars. He'd planned to use my money, which of course he believed he had every right to do." She couldn't hide the bitterness in her tone.

"Whoa, not without talking to you, he didn't," Grady said with a frown. "That's not how marriage is supposed to work. Big financial decisions like that should be made together, with both parties in agreement to the plan."

"Exactly what I said to him. He just shrugged and said the money was a drop in the bucket compared to what I'm worth, and besides, what's mine is his now. He claimed he could do whatever he wanted." She grimaced and looked away. "That's when I knew it was all a lie. That the only reason he'd married me was to get access to my money. It wasn't about me and certainly not about our baby."

Grady slipped his arm around her shoulders, drawing her into a hug. "I'm sorry you had to find out the hard way."

She leaned against him for a moment, inhaling his masculine scent. "Yeah, well, better late than never, right?"

"Right." He pressed a kiss to her temple. "And you got a great kid out of the deal."

She couldn't help but smile. Lifting her head, she gazed up at him, touched by his comments. "Yes, I did. And for that, I have no regrets."

For a long moment, their gazes locked and held. She found it suddenly difficult to breathe, her senses so focused on Grady. She wished she'd married someone like him— strong, sweet, and not looking for financial security in any way.

Unless, of course, she was reading him wrong, too, the way she'd initially believed Nelson's seemingly good intentions.

"I, um, think we need to keep digging into those who knew your ex and his buddy, Bobby Morton," Grady said, interrupting her thoughts.

"Okay." She looked away, hoping her cheeks weren't as red hot as they felt. "Although I'm not sure why Nelson would start coming after Lucy now."

Grady frowned. "The timing is interesting. Can you think of any reason why Nelson would be focused on you at this time? Maybe the heart ball that's coming up to benefit St. Mary's Children's Hospital?"

She shook her head. "I became a spokesperson for the charity after Lucy was born and had to undergo open heart surgery as a result of a birth defect. Nelson and I were separated by then. I made sure to issue the financial separation first, so he couldn't continue to go through my money."

"The jerk," Grady muttered.

She privately agreed. "Our divorce was final just two weeks before his arrest. I wondered if he'd been out drowning his sorrows over our breakup, not that I think he missed anything but the cash flow."

"So this isn't some sort of anniversary?" Grady pressed.

"Nope." She tried to think back to their brief marriage. "I wish I could tell you more. I blocked most of those memories away, refusing to dwell too much on the mistakes I made in the past."

"Smart thinking," he murmured. "I'm surprised he didn't drag the divorce on longer, though."

"My father made Nelson sign a prenup." The fact that Nelson had argued long and hard about the need to sign a legal document prior to their marriage should have been a red flag. Unfortunately, she had waved it off as his way of asking her to trust him. Too bad, the joke was on her, because she couldn't trust Nelson as far as she could throw him across the room. "I sued for full custody of Lucy, and he didn't even argue about it or put up a fight, which frankly surprised me. The best way for him to get access to my money was to sue for joint child support." She sighed. "Of course, his going to jail didn't hurt. The judge granted me sole custody without blinking an eye."

"His loss, Lauren." Grady's compassionate expression was so intensely kind and sweet that it was all she could do not to kiss him. Then, as if he'd read her thoughts, Grady leaned in and brushed his lips against hers.

"Mom, my show is over," Lucy called. Lauren sprang back from Grady so fast she nearly tipped her chair over.

"Coming." Her voice sounded low and hoarse, as if she'd been screaming at one of Lucy's soccer games. Flustered, feeling certain her longing to kiss Grady had been telegraphed on her features, she jumped to her feet, clutching the blanket close as she hurried into the living room to find another show for Lucy to watch.

But the brief kiss she and Grady shared left a tingling sensation on her lips as if she'd touched a live wire. Something that had never happened with Nelson.

More proof that she'd married the wrong man. Now, she just needed to remind herself that Grady was here because she'd hired him through Grayson's Guardians to protect Lucy.

Not because he cared for her on a personal level.

7

―――――

Grady watched Lauren head into the living room to help Lucy find another show to watch. Then he turned to stare blindly at the computer screen. His heart raced as if he'd run a marathon from their brief but electric kiss. Had he imagined the sizzling connection between them, or had Lauren felt it too? He wasn't even sure who had initiated the kiss. All he knew for sure was that he would have loved nothing more than to kiss her again.

But that could not happen. He knew better than to get emotionally involved with a protectee under his care. Especially a single mother with a daughter. If he didn't keep his head clear, he might fail in his mission to protect them. He absolutely needed to stay focused on the threat.

Not how much he was beginning to care for Lauren and her daughter.

He scrubbed his hands over his face, wondering if the lack of sleep was messing with his brain. Not that it mattered. He had a job to do and forced himself to get back to the task at hand, uncovering the source of the threat.

The more he heard about Lauren's ex-husband, the more he loathed the man. Not just because he'd married her for her money, but because of his decision to drive under the influence to the point he'd killed his best friend. Yet Nelson was still in jail. It would not be easy to prove the man was manipulating someone into kidnapping his own daughter.

Not just one person, but two. Which seemed even more unlikely.

He needed to ask Griff to find out if anyone had visited Nelson Derringer in jail recently. Like over the last three to four weeks. All visitors were logged into the system, so that might be a place to start. The washer beeped, indicating the load of clothes were finished, so he crossed over to toss everything into the dryer, then returned to the kitchen. He hated to keep bugging Griff, but he pulled out his phone to make another call.

"Hey, Grady." If Griff was annoyed, he didn't let on. "I've updated Agent David Braun on our conversation. He should be calling you shortly."

"Thanks. I have another favor to ask. Will you please find out if Nelson Derringer has had visitors recently, say in the past few weeks? My theory is that Nelson could be orchestrating the kidnapping attempt from behind bars, promising a big payout once Lauren's father hands over the ransom."

"Great minds think alike," Griff said. "I've requested that information from the correctional facility where he's being held. I'm hoping to hear back soon."

"Thanks." He should have known Griff was on top of things.

"Anything else?" Griff asked.

"Not at the moment." He tapped the mouse pad to bring

the computer screen to life. "I would like to dig into both Bobby Morton and the former security guard, Joe O'Neil. I would have expected the FBI or local law enforcement to have already done that, but I can't just sit here twiddling my thumbs."

"I understand your frustration. Hopefully, you'll learn more when Agent David Braun gets in touch with you."

"Thanks, Griff. I appreciate your help." Grady ended the call, then glanced over to where Lauren was still playing with the remote. He rose, secured the blanket around his waist, and crossed over. "Need help?"

"Yes, please." She gratefully handed over the device. "I don't know why this television seems more complicated than the one we have back home."

"It's a satellite service." He flipped through the menu. "These cabins are too remote for wired cable plans."

"At least it's not just me being an idiot." Lauren flashed a wry smile.

"Never. This service is a little different from the one we use in Wyoming too." He managed to find another kid's station, then handed the remote back. Before he could say anything else, his phone rang.

"Come with me into the kitchen." He held up the phone. "This is FBI Agent David Braun."

"Okay." Lauren followed him back to the oak table.

Grady answered the call. "This is McFarland."

"Grady McFarland? This is Special Agent David Braun from the Chicago office of the FBI." The fed's tone was curt. "I understand there have been new developments in the Ariel Turner abduction?"

Grady thought it was interesting the guy referred to the case as Ariel's abduction, rather than the intended kidnapping of Lucy Chandler. No wonder Lauren had gotten the impression these guys didn't display a sense of urgency. "Yes, I would like to put you on speaker so Lauren can participate in this discussion as well." Without waiting for Braun to respond, he lowered the phone and put the call on speaker. "Agent Braun, have you spoken with the Chicago PD? There was a shooting at Lauren Chandler's apartment early this morning. As we escaped from the penthouse apartment, a dark SUV tried to ram into us. I managed to avoid the collision, but barely. If I'd been in a car with less horsepower, the maneuver might have worked."

"I have a voice message from a Lieutenant Olson," Braun admitted. "Your friend Griff got to me first, so I thought it best to go straight to the source."

Lauren looked skeptical. Grady shrugged, having no idea if Braun was being forthright about his relationship with the local cops or not. "Great, thanks for calling. Prior to the penthouse shooting, my Jeep was targeted by gunfire while I was driving Ms. Chandler and her daughter home. That was between five fifteen and five thirty last evening. Whoever these guys are, they're escalating in their attempt to get to Lucy."

There was a brief silence on the other end of the line. Finally, Braun said, "That does seem to be the case. I know Ms. Chandler believed her daughter was the intended target all along, but we didn't have proof."

"You do now," Lauren said, speaking up for the first time. "Why else would the kidnappers let Ariel go? This is about me and Lucy. Ariel was an innocent victim, taken by mistake, which is why the kidnappers released her."

"I understand," Braun said. "Tell me again about that shooting incident."

Grady explained how the penthouse window was shattered with a bullet and how there was a dark SUV waiting for them as they escaped via the underground parking garage. "There has to be at least two people involved. The shooter and the driver of the SUV."

"I concur," Braun agreed. "From what you're describing, there wasn't enough time to get from an adjacent building where the shooter must have been to take the shot, all the way down to street level to attempt to drive into you."

"We'd like to know if you have any leads," Grady said. "Detective Kramer mentioned a former Savion security guard by the name of Joe O'Neil who was fired nine months ago for theft. He did a brief stint in jail but has been released."

"Joe O'Neil? Do you have a DOB to go with that?" Braun asked.

Annoyed that he was the one providing the federal agent information, Grady reined in his temper and recited the information. "Also, did you look into Lauren's ex-husband, Nelson Derringer? There was a prenup, which limited his ability to get financial support after the divorce. That gives him a pretty good reason to go after Lauren and her daughter."

"We did look at him, but based on this new information, we'll dig a little deeper." Computer keys clicked in the background. "Hmm. This is interesting. It looks like Derringer is scheduled to be released in two months."

"Two months?" Lauren paled. "That can't be right. He still has two years left on his sentence."

"Yeah, but our prisons are overcrowded, and he's likely viewed as a lesser threat to the general public. From what I'm seeing here, Derringer will be released on parole in two months, possibly less," Braun explained. "He'll have to submit to monthly drug and alcohol screenings and wear an ankle monitor so law enforcement can track his movements."

Grady reached over to squeeze Lauren's hand reassuringly, then addressed the phone. "That news only adds credence to our theory that he's somehow pulling strings from inside the joint. Derringer will be back on the street without any means of financial support. Could be he plans to cash in on the ransom."

"I agree." He was glad Braun seemed to take their concern seriously. "We'll look at any connections between Derringer and this O'Neil guy."

"Thank you." Lauren's tone was subdued. He could tell she was already imagining what Nelson might do once he was out of jail. Would he decide to go after Lauren for joint custody of Lucy? He prayed that would not be the case. "Oh, you should be aware that Nelson might be able to support himself," Lauren said. "He was a stockbroker when I met him. I imagine he can try to get back into the game once he's released."

A stockbroker? Grady hadn't known that. He filed the information away for future reference. "I doubt any firm will hire him with a criminal record."

"He could open up his own business," Braun said.

"Yeah, but I'm not sure very many people will be eager to hand over their hard-earned cash to a former convict." Grady sure wouldn't.

"Nelson's former frat buddies might," Lauren said.

She had a point. Some guys tended to stick together. He and his military teammates had done that, despite the horrors of war.

"Where are you now?" Braun asked. "I don't recognize this phone number."

"We're safe," Grady quickly answered, without giving

Lauren a chance to reveal their location. "You can reach us at this number for the time being. If that changes, we'll let you know."

There was another long pause as the fed digested that bit of information. Then Braun said, "Okay, I appreciate the updated information."

Grady would have preferred the information flow to have been the other way around, but there was nothing he could do about that now. "Thanks, Agent Braun. We'll be in touch."

Lauren didn't say anything as he reached over to disconnect from the call. Then she abruptly buried her face in her hands. "I can't believe they're letting him out early."

"I'm sorry." He rested his hand on her shoulder. "The good news is that he'll still be on parole. And that he'll be monitored."

She shook her head, sniffled, then finally looked up at him. "What if—"

"Don't." He shook his head. "There's no point in going down that path. A lot of things can happen over the next few weeks. If we find out Nelson is part of this, he'll face new charges. He could get into a fight or something within the correctional facility too. Even if he does get out, he could do something to break his parole, which would send him back behind bars. Let's just focus on uncovering the source of the danger."

She closed her eyes for a moment, then sighed. "You're right. The current threat is more important than what might happen a few weeks from now."

"Exactly." He smiled reassuringly. "We'll get through this."

She glanced over to where Lucy was watching television. "This is going to sound terrible, but I hope Nelson is the one responsible. Nothing would make me happier than his being kept in jail for the rest of his life."

"I understand." He wished he could reassure her that she had nothing to worry about. But from what little he knew of Derringer, he wouldn't put anything past the guy.

"What are you going to do now?" Lauren asked.

"I'll keep poking around to see what if anything I can find online." He wasn't an expert at investigating cases, but he needed to keep busy. "You and Lucy should relax for a while. I know you didn't get much sleep last night."

"Okay." She hitched up her blanket and stood. "How much longer until the laundry is done?"

He glanced at his watch. "Roughly thirty minutes."

She nodded and moved back into the living room to sit beside her daughter. Grady had to pull his gaze away to focus on the computer. Griff and Agent Braun were looking at Nelson Derringer, so he switched gears to dig into Joe O'Neil. With the DOB Griff had provided, he was able to home in on the guy.

The former Savion security guard was a forty-two-year-old man who did not have military or law enforcement background. Grady found a divorce on file, which was interesting. The timing of the divorce made him think the guy had resorted to theft to deal with his legal bills. Not a smart move since his arrest had only added to his money troubles.

Had O'Neil turned to kidnapping? Anything was possible, but he didn't think the guy would be able to set up somewhere in a nearby building to shoot at him through the penthouse apartment window.

But O'Neil could have been the guy on the road who'd tried to ram into his car. Especially since Joe O'Neil likely knew Nelson Derringer as Lauren's husband.

"Lauren?" He glanced at her over his shoulder. He

winced when she opened her eyes, as if she may have been asleep. "Did you and Nelson live in the penthouse together?"

"Yes." She yawned and rubbed her eyes. Then understanding what he was thinking dawned on her features. "I'm sure Nelson and Joe knew each other, at least on sight." She wrinkled her nose. "Nelson wasn't much for befriending the hired help. He saw them as beneath him. I'm not sure Nelson would have even known Joe's first name."

He nodded. "Okay, that helps."

For the next half hour, he dug through Joe O'Neil's social media without finding anything remotely useful. His thoughts kept going back to Lauren's ex-husband and his upcoming release from jail. When the dryer was finished, he unloaded it and quickly handed Lauren and Lucy their clothing.

As he changed, he tried to imagine what Nelson would do when he got out of jail. And silently admitted he didn't like the idea of being too far away from Lauren to support her when that happened.

Dangerous thoughts. He was there to protect her from a kidnapper, nothing more. Once this case was over, he'd go back to his home in Cody, Wyoming, until Rex Grayson assigned him to something else.

His path and Lauren's would never cross again.

Deeply shaken by the thought of Nelson getting out of prison early, Lauren couldn't concentrate. She had not anticipated that. She'd gone along in her life thinking she had two years before she had to worry about Nelson.

Lucy was still too young and impressionable. What if

Nelson filed a petition to see his daughter? Sure, she could fight him in court, but if he claimed to be a reformed man, determined to be a loving father, she wasn't sure she'd win. Some judges were compelled to allow biological parents to see their child. And it wasn't as if Nelson had ever been abusive toward her. He was just a jerk, plain and simple.

Her chest squeezed painfully at the thought of handing her daughter over to a virtual stranger. What if Nelson had changed for the worse? What if he did something to hurt their daughter?

"Mom? Is something wrong? Why are you crying?" Lucy's question pierced her thoughts.

She quickly swiped at her eyes. "Nothing is wrong, sweetie. I'm just tired. How do you like your show?"

"It's good." Lucy leaned against her as if sensing her mother's sadness. "Grady will keep us safe."

"Yes, he will." She forced herself to sound upbeat and reassuring. The last thing Lucy needed was to live in fear. And her daughter was right about the fact that they were safe here at the cabin with Grady.

"What time can we eat dinner?" Lucy asked. "We're having Captain Jack's, right?"

"Yes. We'll eat soon, okay?" She wrapped her arm around Lucy, hugging her close. She'd figure out how to handle Nelson later. As Grady pointed out, there were other factors that could prevent Nelson from being released. A part of her wanted to pray that Nelson would get into a fight or do something else bad enough that they'd cancel his release. Yet somehow, she didn't think God would appreciate that approach.

Better that she pray for Nelson to find peace and to move on with his life, leaving her and Lucy alone.

Pushing up from the sofa, she headed into the kitchen.

The frozen pizza wouldn't take that long to cook, so she would wait until five thirty to throw it in the oven. She dropped into the chair beside Grady. "Will you help me with something?"

"Of course." Grady instantly turned away from the computer to face her. "What do you need?"

She flushed. "I need you to help me pray. I don't want Nelson to be harmed in any way, but I can't stand the thought of his fighting for joint custody of Lucy." She glanced over to make sure her daughter couldn't hear. "She doesn't even know him. He's a complete stranger to her. I can't just let him have her every other weekend or whatever arrangement the judge allows. I just can't."

"Lauren, don't torture yourself like this." Grady took both of her hands in his. "Nelson isn't even out of jail yet."

"I know that." She bit back a flash of anger. "But hiding my head in the sand isn't going to help either. He's getting out sooner or later. I need to be prepared."

"Okay, you're right. Let's pray." He bowed his head, continuing to hold both of her hands in his. She drew in a deep calming breath and let it out slowly. It took Grady a moment before he cleared his throat and began. "Dear Lord Jesus, we ask You to please protect Lauren and Lucy from danger. We also humbly ask that You lead Nelson down a path to a more fulfilling life. Please show him that the best way to move on is to avoid disrupting his daughter's life in a negative way. We ask this in Jesus's name. Amen."

"Amen." She tightened her grip on Grady's hands. "That was perfect. Thank you."

"Anytime." He searched her gaze for a moment. "I believe in the power of prayer. I hope you continue to lean on your faith to get through this."

"I'm trying." She offered a lopsided smile. "I'm not used to praying like you are."

"Hey, I'm no expert either." He grinned. "The Sullivans taught me everything I know about faith and prayer."

She cocked her head to the side. "Are these the same friends who damaged your house?"

"Yep. There are nine siblings altogether, and they have a search and rescue ranch with highly trained K9s. I went to school with Joel and Justin Sullivan. They're twins. We lost touch for a while when I was in the army but reconnected after I got out."

"Nine siblings?" Her eyes widened in shock. "I can't imagine their poor mother, giving birth to nine babies."

"I hear you. They lost their parents over six years ago now, and every single one of them is married. All within the past year or so," he added wryly. "Kinda amazing when you think about it."

She was still trying to imagine giving birth nine times. "Well, I'm glad you have friends like them."

He looked like he was about to say something but changed his mind. He released her hands and stood. "Do you want me to throw the pizzas into the oven?"

"I can do it." She gestured to the computer. "Have you found anything interesting?"

"Not really." He grimaced. "I've been combing through O'Neil's social media. There's nothing to suggest he's friends or acquaintances with Nelson."

"They wouldn't be friends." She knew there was no way Nelson would allow his frat buddies to see him befriending a lowly security guard. Former security guard. "Maybe we should look at Nelson's other friends from the fraternity. Maybe one of them is helping him with these attempts against us."

"Maybe. Do you know what frat he was a part of?" Grady sat and turned the computer toward her. "If you can find the right one, I can ask Griff to get us a list of names."

She frowned, leaning forward. "I think it was the Delta Sigma Chi fraternity." She typed the information into the search bar, adding Chicago Loyola University to narrow the field. The picture of a frat house bloomed on the screen. She tapped it with an index finger. "Yes, it's this one. Nelson has a picture of him and his buddies standing outside the building."

"That's a good place to start." He bookmarked the page. "Can you remember any of their names?"

"Other than Bobby Morton?" She thought back to her short marriage. Nelson had mentioned them, but she hadn't paid much attention at the time. She remembered thinking Nelson was spending too much time talking about the glory days of his past, rather than being focused on the present. Especially his new wife. "I'm sorry. Nothing comes to mind."

"That's okay." Grady shrugged. "When Griff calls, I'll get the list. Maybe seeing a name written down will spark a memory."

"Okay." She glanced at her watch and stood. "I'll throw the pizzas into the oven. It's early, but I know Lucy is hungry."

"I am too," he teased. "Thanks."

It took her a few minutes to figure out how to work the oven. It wasn't that she was clueless, it was just that she was accustomed to the newer appliances they had. This oven looked as if it were thirty years old or more. Not that she was complaining. She was grateful to be in the isolated and rustic cabin with Lucy.

And Grady.

While the oven preheated, she read the directions on the

back of the frozen pizza box. Feeling Grady's gaze on her, she flushed and quickly unwrapped them. They looked a little like cardboard to her, but Lucy loved them, which was all that mattered.

When Grady's phone rang, she whirled to face him.

"It's Griff," he said, before answering the call.

"Put it on speaker," she whispered, crossing over to join him. Lucy was still enthralled with her movie, which was a good thing.

"Hey, Griff, I'm putting you on speaker so Lauren can hear this." Grady lowered the phone to the table. "We spoke to Agent David Braun. He seems to be on board with continuing the investigation."

"That's good. I'm not sure why he was taking such a laid-back approach anyway."

She arched a brow and shrugged. Grady nodded. "We aren't sure either. When we told him about the gunfire incidents, though, he changed his tune. Did you find anything new?"

"Yeah, that's why I'm calling. I have two names for you. Both of these people visited Nelson Derringer at the correctional institute over the past six weeks. Other than his lawyer, who was only there once from what I can see."

"Two names?" Lauren's heart filled with hope. "Who are they?"

"A woman by the name of Karla Dalton and a man by the name of Eric Howington. Do either of those names ring a bell?"

"No, they don't." She frowned, then asked, "I'm surprised a woman visited him."

"Actually, she visits on a weekly basis," Griff said. "I'm wondering if they're romantically involved in some way."

Romantically involved? She stared at Grady. "I hope they are. Maybe that's an indication he's moved on."

"Or he's charmed this Karla into helping him," Grady said, deflating her balloon of hope. "Have you run their backgrounds?"

"Yes, neither of them has a criminal background. That doesn't rule them out as being involved, though," Griff hastily added. "I think they bear looking into."

Lauren sat back in her chair, her mind whirling. Was it possible Karla and Eric were working together in this kidnapping plan? If so, she hoped they were found and arrested very soon.

Before Nelson was released from jail.

8

———

For Lauren's sake, Grady hoped Nelson was romantically involved with this Karla woman. Deep down, he couldn't help but wonder if Nelson was manipulating the woman. Maybe pretending to care so that she would help him orchestrate these attempts to kidnap Lucy.

Eric Howington could easily be involved too.

"Do you know if Eric Howington was in Nelson's fraternity at Loyola?" He held Lauren's gaze. "We know Nelson's dead friend, Bobby Morton, went to college with him."

"Hang on, I'll check." He could hear Griff typing on a computer. "No, it doesn't look like Howington was part of a fraternity."

Grady turned to Lauren. "Any idea how Eric and Nelson may have met?"

She shook her head, her expression troubled. "I'm sorry, but I have no idea. If Eric isn't a friend from college, maybe from work?"

"Griff, can you get us a list of all the members of the

Delta Sigma Chi fraternity? Nelson Derringer was a member, and we'd like to see who else might be involved."

"Makes sense. I'll ask Dom to get the list for us," Griff agreed. "I don't see anything that indicates Howington and Nelson worked together, though."

Grady frowned. "That's odd. It takes a dedicated friend to visit someone in jail. Usually people distance themselves from that sort of thing."

"I agree," Griff said. "Eric visited him twice in the past month."

Grady could tell Lauren thought Eric was involved in the attacks. "Okay, thanks. What else do we know about Karla Dalton? Maybe the local cops should interview her."

"I don't know much yet, but interviewing her is a good idea. I'd almost rather the FBI took the lead on that, though," Griff said. "Nothing against the Chicago PD, but we wouldn't want to tip our hand on our suspicions."

"Could Eric and Kayla be working together somehow?" Lauren asked. "I mean, maybe Eric is the gunman, and Karla is the driver."

"Anything is possible, but without proof, all we can do is talk to them," Griff said. "Do you want me to touch base with Agent Braun?"

"We can do that." Grady felt bad dragging Griff into the investigation. "I don't want you to get in trouble for this."

"I'm just helping a friend," Griff said lightly. "There's only so much investigating I can do from Wyoming."

"True." He shrugged and looked at Lauren. "Do you have any other questions for Griff?"

"This is going to sound weird, but do you have a picture of Karla?" Lauren flushed. "Maybe I'll recognize her."

"Good point." Griff tapped the keyboard again. "Okay,

I'm sending photos of both Eric Howington and Karla Dalton."

Grady pulled up his email address and waited for the pictures to load. Karla's came up first. He turned the laptop so Lauren could see the screen. The woman was pretty enough, but nothing special. Not nearly as beautiful as Lauren.

Lauren stared at the photo for several long seconds. Then she sighed and shook her head. "I don't recognize her."

"Okay, let's try Eric." He double-tapped the mouse pad to bring up the second image. Eric looked a little rough around the edges; there was a hardness to the guy's eyes that gave Grady the sense he'd done some bad things. Considering his criminal record was clean, either the guy was just having a rough day or he'd been smart enough to avoid being caught.

"I'm sorry, I don't recognize him either." Lauren looked frustrated. "I wish I knew where Nelson met both of these people."

"Talk to Agent Braun," Griff said. "Once he interviews them, he may be able to shed some light on that for you."

"Thanks, Griff. And please don't forget to send that fraternity list."

"Will do. Dom's working on that now. He should have an email sent to you within the hour." Griff disconnected from the line.

Lauren reached over to enlarge Karla's picture. It was a rather unflattering driver's license photo. "I don't know what to think about her. It's hard for me to understand why any woman would choose to get involved with someone who was serving time for manslaughter."

"I'm sure they were involved prior to his arrest." Grady

nodded at the screen. "Unless she's one of those women who are fascinated by prisoners."

Lauren wrinkled her nose. "I personally don't get the appeal. Why not cut her losses and find someone else? Nelson is not worth waiting for."

He wasn't sure what to say to that. Lauren knew Nelson better than anyone, having been married to the guy. It was possible Nelson had changed since their divorce, but he doubted it. "We'll call Agent Braun next. Maybe she's hanging onto Nelson because she's helping him with these attacks in exchange for a big payout."

"Good idea." Lauren minimized the photo and sat back. He reached over to pick up the phone to make the call. He put the call on speaker so Lauren could participate too. This time, Agent Braun answered the call, rather than sending it to voice mail.

"Braun."

"Agent Braun, this is Grady McFarland. We spoke earlier. I'm here with Lauren Chandler. We have you on speaker. We recently learned two people have visited Lauren's ex-husband in jail over the past few weeks." He quickly gave the FBI agent the details Griff had given them. "Lauren doesn't recognize either of these individuals. She hasn't been close to her ex since their divorce."

"How did you get this information?" Braun asked.

"Through a friend." Grady knew the federal agent could probably figure out they'd gotten the intel through Griff. "We understand these individuals don't have a criminal record, but we think it's worth interviewing them."

"Oh, you do, huh?" There was no mistaking the sarcasm in Braun's tone. "What makes you think they haven't already been interviewed?"

Grady arched a brow at Lauren. "I guess I'd have

expected you to mention that when you updated us on the case."

Braun sighed loudly. "Okay, look, I appreciate your efforts to help. But we're handling the investigation. All you need to do is to stay low and out of harm's way until we have this guy behind bars."

"Excuse me, Agent Braun, but it's my daughter's life that's on the line." Despite the polite words, Lauren's voice was sharp. "If you think I'm just going to sit back and do nothing, you're sadly mistaken. If I need to escalate my concerns to the governor or our state senators, I will gladly make some calls."

Grady smiled encouragingly, then added, "Lauren has put her life on hold because of this, and Lucy is missing school. This has already gone on for longer than it should. I expect you to update us with the results of the interviews."

Braun was silent for a moment, as if he was remembering how wealthy Lauren was. "Okay, fine, I'll update you as soon as I have more information to share."

Braun's vague response made it clear the interviews had not been done. Grady managed not to mention that and simply thanked the agent and disconnected from the call.

"Maybe I should make some calls to the politicians my father supported." Lauren's expression was troubled. "I knew they didn't seem to be moving on this case with a sense of urgency, but Agent Braun's attitude made me want to smack him."

"I understand, and I think you made your position on this loud and clear." He reached over to take her hand. "I'm sure they'll follow through with the interviews. Don't worry. Now, I think the pizzas are probably done."

Her blue eyes widened in horror as she jumped to her feet. "I forgot all about them!"

"It's okay." He rose and quickly took the hot pads from her hands. The pizzas were golden brown, not burned. He grinned and pulled them out. "See? They're perfect."

She flushed and shook her head. "You must think I'm lame."

"Not at all." He knew she could do everyday things. It was more likely that she wasn't accustomed to doing them.

Lauren smiled ruefully, then called to her daughter. "Lucy, time to eat."

"Aw, Mom, my show is still on!"

"I thought Captain Jack's was your favorite?" Lauren asked.

"It is!" Lucy tore her gaze from the television, then scrambled off the sofa. "Okay, I'm coming."

He cut the pizza into slices, thinking how ironic it was that a kid would choose a frozen store-bought pizza over the Chicago deep dish the city was famous for.

Bringing the pizza to the table, he closed the laptop and set it aside. His attempts to investigate the case on his own weren't going as well as he'd hoped. So far, it was only through Griff that they'd gotten anything useful.

"I'd like to say grace," he said, when Lucy had finished washing her hands at the sink. Lucy glanced at her mother but didn't argue.

"Bow your head, Lucy," Lauren said.

He cleared his throat. "Dear Lord Jesus, we thank You for this food we are about to eat. We also continue to ask You to keep us all safe in Your care. Amen."

"Amen," Lauren and Lucy echoed.

He waited for Lauren and Lucy to take what they wanted first, before digging in to his own pizza. For something they'd picked out of a grocery store freezer, it wasn't terrible. He smiled at Lucy. "I can see why this is your favorite."

Lauren shot him a skeptical look, but simply added, "It's good, isn't it, Lucy?"

The little girl nodded, her mouth full of pepperoni pizza. Grady was glad Lucy had gotten some playtime, building a snowman, then watching TV. He hoped the fear of the gunfire had faded so that she wouldn't suffer more nightmares.

When they finished eating, Lucy darted back into the living room. "Mom, can you help find my show?"

"Normally, I don't allow her to watch this much television," Lauren said in a low voice. "Too much screen time isn't good for kids."

"I know, but this is an extenuating circumstance, don't you think?" He stacked their plates and carried them to the sink. Their lunch dishes were still there too.

"Yes, I do." She joined him, watching as he filled one side of the sink with warm sudsy water and went to work. "I can do the dishes."

"So can I." He grinned. "I bet I have more KP experience than you do."

"KP?" She frowned. "Kitchen, what?"

"Kitchen patrol. The army loves its acronyms." He nodded at the dishtowel. "You can dry and put away."

They worked together in silence for a few minutes, before Lauren asked, "Do you think Karla is one of the people involved in these attempts?"

He shrugged. "As Griff said, anything is possible. I served with some women, not many, but they were good soldiers."

She nodded thoughtfully. "I really want to believe a woman wouldn't kidnap someone's daughter, but if she's not a mother, she may not realize the agony she's causing."

"Or she doesn't care because in her mind, the end justifies the means." He tried to smile reassuringly. "Don't dwell on this, Lauren. If she's involved, the police will find the evidence they need and arrest her."

"I hope you're right about that." She dried the plates and put them away. "They've escaped being caught so far."

He hated to admit she was right. "With all the cameras in the city, I'm surprised they didn't get something more from the initial abduction."

"Me too." She glanced over at Lucy. He noticed the little girl was wrapped in a blanket, her eyes drooping with fatigue. "Maybe by tomorrow this will be over."

"I hope so." If Karla and/or Eric Howington were involved, it shouldn't be too difficult to track their movements over the past twenty-four hours. And there was still Joe O'Neil, the former security guard of Savion Enterprises to consider. They had more now than when they'd started, which was encouraging.

When he finished washing the dishes, Grady moved back to the kitchen table. A few keystrokes later, he found the list of fraternity members from the few years Nelson had been there. The list was longer than he anticipated, and he hoped Lauren would be able to identify someone who they could zero in on.

If not? He'd methodically start digging into each of the names, himself. Besides, it wasn't as if he planned to get much sleep. A few military combat naps at the most was all he could afford.

Grady needed to stay alert and on guard until the kidnapper was caught dand safely behind bars.

WHEN THE DISHES were dry and put away, Lauren crossed over to join Grady. He glanced at her, then gestured to the screen. "Here's the list. Can you point out Nelson's friends? I figure they're the logical place to start."

She stifled a yawn and sat beside him. "I'll do my best." The list of fraternity members was long, as it spanned several years. She rubbed her eyes, then began to read.

"Here's one, Archer Bloom." She continued reading as Grady made a note of the name. The list was in alphabetical order, and she quickly passed her ex-husband's name, searching her memory for more tidbits from their brief marriage. "Jack Henry is another."

"You're doing great," Grady said.

She appreciated his attempt to sound positive. The truth was that they had no idea if any of these former fraternity brothers of Nelson's were involved. After hearing how Eric Howington and Karla Dalton had visited her ex while his was in prison, something she was convinced these frat boys would never do, she felt certain Eric and Karla should be put higher on the suspect list. These frat brothers had probably all moved on with their lives and wanted nothing to do with a loser like Nelson.

She frowned when she passed Bobby Morton's name. The poor guy had paid the ultimate price of being Nelson's friend. Granted, Bobby had gotten in the car with her ex that fateful night, despite how they'd both been drinking. Bobby could have chosen to walk or take a rideshare. Shaking off the memories, she pushed on. "Andrew Salzburg, Nelson called him Drew." She continued down the list until she got to the end. With a sigh, she sat back in the chair. "I'm sorry. I only recall these three names. There could be others. I just didn't pay attention when Nelson talked about them."

"Hey, three names are better than none." Grady smiled

and tapped the screen. "I'll start with these. Maybe something will pop."

"I hope so." She wanted to do her part in bringing this nightmare to an end. Then another wide yawn caught her off guard.

"Hey, I think it's time you and Lucy get some sleep." Grady rested a hand on her shoulder. "You look beat. Take the bedroom. I'll stay out here."

She wanted to point out that the arrangement hadn't worked so well when he'd stayed in the living room of the penthouse apartment. Then again, they'd been safe here at the cabin. The only near miss had been when they'd almost driven past a cop in their stolen car. Grady's altering the plates with black tape should provide another level of protection.

She hoped.

When Grady continued to look at her, she forced a nod. There was no point in fighting the inevitable. "Okay. But I think you should get some sleep too."

"I will." He nodded toward the bedrooms. "Make yourself comfortable."

Glancing at Lucy, who was fighting to keep her eyes open long enough to finish the show, she nodded and rose. "Time for bed, Lucy."

"Aw, Mom." Her daughter's protest was weak. "My show is almost over."

"Let's see." She sat down on the sofa next to Lucy. Eyeing the show, she realized her daughter was right. It was nearly over. "Okay, looks like it will be ending in about five minutes or so."

"Thanks, Mom." Lucy snuggled beside her. And before the five-minute timeline was up, the little girl fell asleep.

She was about to ease away from Lucy when Grady

came to the rescue. He crossed over, keeping his voice low. "I'll carry her."

"Thanks," she whispered as he lifted Lucy from the sofa. Much like in the middle of the night, he brought her blanket along with her. Lauren struggled to her feet, hoping Lucy wouldn't wake up. Thankfully, Lucy didn't stir as Grady carried her down the hall to the bedrooms. She moved ahead to pull the covers down on one of the twin beds. "Set her here."

Grady did so, and for a moment, Lucy looked like she might wake up. Lauren pulled the covers up, and Lucy relaxed against the pillow.

"Thanks," she whispered as Grady stepped back into the hallway.

"Anytime." He glanced past her. "I promise nobody will get to her while I'm here."

"I know." She believed him. She stared up at him, wishing for something she couldn't have before forcing herself to turn away. "Good night, Grady."

"Good night." His voice was low and husky, and it was all she could do not to throw herself into his arms.

After using the bathroom, she crawled into the second twin bed in Lucy's room. She wanted to be close in case her daughter had another nightmare. Or if something else happened. And because of the latter possibility, she stretched out under the covers fully dressed.

For several minutes, she listened to Lucy's even breathing, her thoughts whirling. The possibilities were endless. Karla was either Nelson's girlfriend or helping him in the scheme to kidnap Lucy. Or maybe Eric Howington was the one who was shooting at them. And what about Joe O'Neil, the fired security guard?

When she couldn't take her racing thoughts for another

second, she closed her eyes and focused on prayer. That worked because the next thing she knew, she abruptly awoke, blinking in the darkness.

A sound? Lucy? She lifted herself up on one elbow, glancing over at the twin bed along the wall. Lucy wasn't crying or making any sound. Then what had woken her?

"Lauren?" Grady's low whisper had her pushing the covers aside and rising to her feet. It was so dark here compared to the city. No lights from buildings or cars. She couldn't see anything in the darkness. But then she noticed the breadth of Grady's shoulders as he hovered in the doorway.

"Coming." She tiptoed across the room. As they stepped back from the doorway, she tried to read his expression. "What's wrong?"

"I saw a police car while I was walking the perimeter." The way he said "walking the perimeter" made her think that was another military phrase. "I'm concerned they're homing in on our stolen car."

She sucked in a quick breath. "You changed the plate, though, right?"

"Yeah, but with only one letter and number different, it may not be enough." He grimaced. "I think we should hit the road sooner than later."

Hit the road? She swallowed a protest. The cabin was the first place she'd felt safe since leaving Chicago. She didn't want to leave.

But she didn't want Grady to be arrested for stealing a car either.

"I know it's still early, but I don't want to wait too long," Grady said.

She was surprised to realize the time was five o'clock in the morning. She wondered how much sleep, if any, Grady had gotten. She'd awoken feeling better, until he'd mentioned the need to leave. "How is driving around in a stolen car any safer?"

"It's not, but I have already spoken to my boss. Rex is going to have a rental car waiting for us in Madison."

"Okay." She decided there was no point in arguing. He'd obviously waited to wake her until he had a solid plan. "Do you want me to wake Lucy now, then?"

"Yeah, but first I have a question." His gaze held hers. "Did you know Bobby Morton has a first cousin by the name of Randy Morton?"

Her jaw dropped. "No. I had no idea."

"You didn't meet him? Even at the funeral?" Grady pressed.

"No, I never met him." Her cheeks flushed. "I, uh, didn't attend the funeral. I mean, I would have paid my respects to the Morton family for their loss, but I wasn't so sure Bobby's parents wanted to see me. Not after my soon-to-be ex-husband had recklessly killed their son."

"Okay, that makes sense. But if you ask me, I think Randy Morton also deserves to be investigated. Maybe his way of seeking revenge on your ex is to kidnap your daughter."

She nodded slowly. "If I had known Bobby had a cousin . . ." Then she abruptly stopped herself. "Wait a minute, why didn't Lieutenant Olson or Detective Kramer mention him? Surely they knew Bobby had a cousin with the same name."

"That's a good question." Grady scowled. "Maybe they've already cleared him as a suspect, I'm not sure. But they should have mentioned him."

Once again, she was concerned the local police didn't have the expertise to investigate this. And what about the

FBI? Agent Braun should have known Bobby had a cousin. Yet nobody had mentioned him as a possible suspect.

"I don't like this, Grady. It feels like they're all hiding something from me." She shivered in the darkness. The warmth of the fire had faded, leaving a distinct chill in the air. "Either that, or they're all grossly incompetent."

"Let's give them the benefit of the doubt," Grady said. "I understand and share your concerns. I'm not happy about learning this information on my own either. Once we're safe, we'll follow up with FBI Agent David Braun again." He offered a wan smile. "You may have to make good on your threat to go up the chain of command."

"I have no problem with that." She would do whatever was necessary to protect her daughter. She glanced back at the bedroom, then sighed. "You really want to leave now while it's dark? We could wait until Lucy wakes up."

"I think the sooner we get away from this cabin rental, the better." He wrapped his arm around her shoulder, giving her a brief hug. "Get your coat and Lucy's too. Once she's ready, I'll carry Lucy to the car."

"Okay." She decided not to question his judgment. She headed into the main living space and pulled on her long coat. Then she grabbed Lucy's shoes, tucking them in a grocery bag. She headed back to the bedroom with Lucy's coat and boots.

"Noo," Lucy whined when she shook her daughter awake. "Leave me alone."

"Come on, Lucy. We're going to drive to a new city." She managed to thrust one of her daughter's arms into the coat. "Please, Lucy. We need to go."

"No! Leave me alone!" Her daughter kicked her feet, making it impossible for her to slip on the boots.

"Lucy, stop it. We need to go right now." Grady's deep

voice did the trick. Lucy stopped fighting, looking up at him with a frown.

"Why?" Lucy asked the question but didn't resist when Lauren put her other arm in the coat sleeve and zipped it up. Then she slid both boots onto her daughter's feet.

"Because it's not safe to stay here." Grady scooped Lucy into his arms and strode through the cabin. Lauren didn't see the computer on the table. Presumably, Grady already had it out in the car, as the vehicle was running and ready to go.

It didn't take long to reach the highway. They were headed southwest when she spotted twin headlights growing brighter as a car approached. Moments later, she saw the light bar across the top and grabbed Grady's arm. "It's a cop!"

"I see it." Grady's muscle tightened beneath her fingertips. When the light bar flashed on, red and blue lights swirling, she gasped, overwhelmed by a sense of dread.

This was it. They were heading to jail. She closed her eyes and prayed for God to protect them.

9

———

Tightening his grip on the steering wheel, Grady mentally reviewed what he'd say to the police officer when they were pulled over. Not that the cop would likely be interested in his side of the story once it became clear Grady had hot-wired the car. Maybe he could call Griff to help explain the situation they were in. Especially since he knew Lauren would want to pay for the owner's car anyway.

Then the police cruiser whipped past them. He blew out his breath, looking over at Lauren in shock. Shifting his gaze to the rearview mirror, he wondered if the cop would turn around to come at them from behind.

But he didn't. Instead, the squad disappeared around the bend. Because of the early hour, the red and blue lights still lit up the sky, but eventually, they faded away as well.

"I don't understand," Lauren whispered. "Where did he go?"

"No idea." He flexed his fingers. "I'm just glad he didn't come after us."

"Why are we hiding from the police?" Lucy asked. "You

told me that if I'm ever scared and alone to run to the closest police officer."

"We're not hiding from the police," Lauren said. Grady arched a brow, because the truth was they absolutely were hiding from the cops because of the stolen car. She turned in her seat to smile at her daughter. "We didn't want to be stopped because that would take extra time, and we want to get to the new city as soon as possible."

"But if I'm alone and scared, I should still go to a policeman for help, right?" Lucy asked. Grady realized this must have been a conversation between mother and daughter after Ariel's abduction.

"Yes, absolutely. The police are the good guys," Lauren said firmly. "You can always run to them for help."

"Okay." Lucy seemed to buy that answer. Then she asked, "Why do we have to go to a new city?"

"You remember Mr. Rex Grayson, right?" Grady caught Lucy's gaze in the rearview mirror. "He's arranging for us to have a different car, but we have to get to a city called Madison to pick it up."

"What's wrong with this car?" Lucy asked.

"Nothing is wrong, but we borrowed it for a little while, and the owner wants it back." Lauren's brow furrowed as she expanded on their fib. "That's why we asked Mr. Rex for a different car."

"Okay." Lucy yawned, then said, "I need to go to the bathroom."

Of course she did. Grady swallowed a groan. He should have realized that and had her use the bathroom prior to leaving the cabin. He glanced at Lauren. "We'll pull off at the next gas station."

"Sounds good." Lauren turned to look at Lucy. "Can you hold it for a few minutes?"

The little girl nodded, but the way she squirmed in her seat was not reassuring. Grady didn't want to have to stop for more clothes if she had an accident. He pushed the speed limit, relieved when he saw they were approaching a small town.

"Almost there," he said encouragingly.

He slowed and turned into the gas station parking lot. He'd barely gotten the car shifted into park when Lucy had her seatbelt off and was getting out of the car. Lauren pushed out, too, and together they hurried inside. He pulled up to the nearest pump, then followed them inside. He smiled at the attendant and pulled cash from his wallet. "Twenty dollars on pump number two."

"Got it." The clerk opened the register, then unlocked the pump. He hurried outside to fill up the tank, hoping the twenty dollars would get them all the way to Madison. When he'd spoken to Rex earlier, he'd mentioned the need for more cash, as well as a clean car, complete with a booster seat for Lucy. Rex had agreed to make the vehicle arrangements and to transfer funds into his account via a cash app. Grady would then need to find a bank to do a withdrawal. The solution wasn't perfect, he'd rather stay completely off-grid, but with Rex being in Chicago, this was the best they could do.

When he finished filling the tank, he headed back inside. Lucy and Lauren were just coming out of the bathroom. "I don't see much to eat," Lauren whispered.

"I know." This gas station wasn't as nice as the last one. There wasn't even fresh coffee available. "Let's just get out of here."

Lauren understood he didn't want to linger. "Come on, Lucy, we need to get back out to the car."

"But I'm hungry," Lucy whined as they headed outside.

"We'll find a place to stop for breakfast soon," he promised as he opened the back door. "What's your favorite breakfast meal?"

"Strawberry waffles," Lucy said without hesitation.

He noticed Lauren wince, but he nodded. "Great, we'll find a breakfast restaurant that serves strawberry waffles."

"Yummy," Lucy said with a wide smile. To her credit, Lauren didn't protest. There was a time and a place to worry about eating healthy, and being on the run from gunmen was not one of them. His goal was to keep Lucy happy as they made their way across the state.

"You can't just give her whatever she wants," Lauren said in a low voice.

He shrugged, glancing at her as he headed back out to the highway. "These are extenuating circumstances."

She sighed. "I know."

The early morning hour worked to their advantage. After the cop had passed them, red and blue lights flashing, there hadn't been much traffic. He was relieved, as it was easy enough to spot a potential tail when they were alone on the highway.

Yet he also knew that would change as the sun came up and citizens headed out to work. He kept a wary eye on the road behind them in case the gas station clerk had noticed their stolen car and reported it. An unlikely scenario, but he couldn't relax until he knew they'd gotten the new rental.

Big cities like Chicago and Milwaukee had police cameras mounted on key intersections for the sole purpose of reading license plates to identify stolen vehicles. But smaller towns did not. Madison was the state capital, so he was pretty sure they had the camera technology.

Would his black electrical tape help hide them as they entered Madison? He hoped so.

"Looks like there's a family restaurant up ahead," Lauren said, breaking into his thoughts.

He nodded. "That works." He caught Lucy's gaze in the rearview mirror. "Ready for breakfast?"

"Yes." Lucy looked happy to hear they were stopping soon.

They'd made good time since leaving the gas station. Yet with dawn rising on the horizon, the traffic around them increased. He didn't see how anyone could have followed them, but he looked at every dark SUV with suspicion. Soon, they approached a small town by the name of Wild Prairie located about seven miles outside Madison. He wasn't sure if the rental car agency would open early, so they might as well linger here at the restaurant for at least an hour or two before rushing into the city.

If their stolen car triggered those police cameras, which he thought was highly likely, they wouldn't have much time before the cops were on them.

"We're here, Lucy. Keep in mind, they may not have strawberry waffles," Lauren warned as he exited the highway and pulled into the restaurant parking lot. "You may have to have pancakes or plain waffles instead."

"They will." Lucy didn't sound concerned. "Ariel and I love eating strawberry waffles."

Lauren rolled her eyes as she unclipped her seatbelt. Grady had the impression Lauren hadn't realized what sorts of foods Lucy ate while spending time at her friend's house.

He pushed out of the car and quickly rounded the front to stay close. He scanned the area but didn't see anything unusual.

So far, so good, he thought grimly as he held the door open for Lauren and Lucy.

The tantalizing aroma of coffee greeted them upon

entering the restaurant. A sign indicated they should seat themselves, so he chose a booth near the back. There weren't many patrons at this hour, the dining room was wide open. He positioned himself so he could see both the main entrance and the side hallway where the restrooms were located.

A young woman came with menus and three water glasses a minute later. "Good morning, my name is Dee, I'll be your server. Would anyone like coffee or tea?"

"Coffee, please," he and Lauren answered at the same time. Dee smiled, and Grady knew she assumed they were a family.

That was what Lauren had wanted, right? A pretend fiancé? He told himself not to think about how wealthy Lauren was.

"Mom, can I have chocolate milk?" Lucy asked. Grady could tell by Lauren's narrowed expression that Lucy was pushing the limits of her patience. "Please?"

Lauren sighed and relented. "Fine. One glass of chocolate milk, please."

"Coming right up." Dee filled their coffee mugs, then left to fetch the milk.

Cradling the mug in his hands, he eyed Lauren as he took a sip of the strong brew. "We may be here a while."

She nodded in understanding and opened the menu. "Lucy, they have blueberry pancakes and waffles. Not strawberry."

"I like blueberries," Lucy said with enthusiasm. "Can we ask for whipped cream on the waffles?"

"We'll see." Lauren reached for her coffee and lowered her voice. "Grady, are we okay money-wise?"

"Yep." They were running low, but they only needed enough cash to get them through the next couple of hours.

He smiled reassuringly. "Don't worry. Order whatever you like."

She nodded and looked back down at the menu. When Dee returned with Lucy's chocolate milk, they placed their order. He went with a farmer's omelet while she had two eggs over easy with toast. Lucy was ecstatic to have her blueberry waffles with whipped cream.

He finished his coffee, then stood. "I'm going back outside to get the computer."

"Okay." Lauren turned her attention to Lucy. "Save some of your chocolate milk for when your meal arrives."

Grady was back in the booth a few minutes later. Lucy had crayons and was coloring on a piece of paper that Dee must have provided. His coffee cup had been refilled too.

"What are you looking at?" Lauren asked as he opened the laptop. "Did you find anything useful last night?"

"I found a criminal record from two years ago on Archer Bloom for drug possession." He shrugged. "Not sure that means he's helping Nelson, but it's possible."

"Hard drugs?" Lauren asked with a frown.

"Yeah. Cocaine." He eyed her over the top of the computer. "Did Nelson do drugs?"

"Not that I'm aware of." She grimaced. "Although as it turned out, I didn't know him as well as I thought I did."

He nodded, then turned back to the computer. "I didn't find any criminal records on his other frat brothers, not even an underage drinking ticket from their college days."

"I guess that's sort of good." She stared down at her coffee cup for a long moment. "I keep thinking of that woman, Karla. Nelson could be charming when he wanted to be. The more I think about these attempts, the more I lean toward believing she's involved."

"Hopefully, we'll hear more from Agent Braun soon." If

they didn't, Grady had no doubt Lauren would follow through on her threat of contacting the governor and other political leaders of the state to get things moving. "My next plan is to check their social media sites to see if that gives us any clues as to what these guys are up to."

"I'm sure they're not so stupid as to post something like that," she scoffed.

"Not a blatant post," he agreed. "But there could be group photos of these guys hanging out together."

She nodded thoughtfully. "Good point."

He reached over to take her hand. "Lauren, we're going to get to through this."

"I know." She squeezed his fingers. "Thank you, Grady."

"Anytime." This was the job she'd hired him to do. Yet he also knew that he was allowing Lauren and Lucy to get too close on a personal level.

He'd never forgive himself if he failed to protect them.

LAUREN CLUNG to Grady's hand for a long moment. When Dee arrived with their meals, she had little choice but to release him. Flustered, she looked away, fearing her growing feelings for Grady were clearly etched on her features.

This was a temporary arrangement. Despite her request to pretend they were engaged, she knew her world and Grady's would never mesh. Yet the more time she spent with him, the more she couldn't help comparing him to her worthless ex-husband.

Any man would be better than Nelson. But she had no interest in dating any of the men in her social circle. Even those who had plenty of money of their own left her cold.

"Looks yummy." Lucy lowered her head to swipe a dollop of whipped cream.

"Hold on, Lucy. We need to say grace." She glanced over to where Grady was watching her daughter's antics with amusement. "Grady?"

He nodded and bowed his head. "Dear Lord Jesus, we ask You to bless this food we are about to eat. We ask again that You please protect us from those who would do us harm. In Jesus's name. Amen."

"Amen," she and Lucy echoed.

"I don't understand why we pray," Lucy said, then she licked another dollop of whipped cream. "We're paying for the food, right?"

"Right." She glanced helplessly at Grady. "We're very fortunate to have money to pay for our meal. Not everyone does."

Lucy scrunched up her forehead. "So if they pray, God gives them food?"

"I think the point is that we need to thank God for what we have." She wasn't an expert on faith. Jesus had fed the poor and hungry, but mentioning that may confuse the issue.

"Your mom is right; we are blessed to have money to pay for our meal. And we need to thank our Lord for keeping us safe." Grady smiled at Lucy. "Look at how long we've been able to stay away from the bad guys. That's partially because our Lord and Savior is always listening to our prayers."

"But I don't see God. Do you?" Lucy asked.

"No, but I can feel Him in my heart." Grady put his hand on his chest. "If you pray, you'll feel Him too."

Lucy didn't look convinced but dropped the subject to dig in to her waffles. Lauren tried not to sigh as her daughter ate the whipped cream first, before trying the waffle itself.

Grady's farmer's omelet was huge; she was glad she hadn't ordered something similar.

Her eggs were good, and they ate in silence for a few minutes. Dee came and refilled their coffee mugs. When Grady finished eating, he reached over and opened the laptop, clearly intending to go back to work.

"What time do you want to head into Madison?" She glanced over to where Lucy was still eating her waffles. Coloring aside, she knew her daughter would get bored if he really intended to sit there for a while.

"I'm checking the rental agency's hours of operation now." His gaze remained focused on the screen. With his thick dark tousled hair and the shadow of his beard darkening his jaw, he looked incredibly attractive.

Completely different from the men she normally associated with. And maybe that was the reason she was so drawn to him. He was different, in a good way, from the men she knew. Then she frowned, abruptly realizing that if her daughter hadn't been targeted by a kidnapper who'd taken the wrong girl, she never would have met him.

Divine intervention? No, that didn't seem right. She was the one who'd gone to Grayson's Guardians to hire him based on her father's recommendation. She was reading too much into the past thirty-six hours they'd been together.

Time to focus on the present. They'd managed to escape the kidnapping threat thus far, but they still needed the police and FBI to do their part to find the men or women responsible. And if they didn't get cracking soon, she'd climb up the chain of command to add pressure.

"Okay, looks like we need to stay here a few minutes longer," Grady said. "The rental agency opens at seven thirty."

That was only a half hour from now. She stacked her

empty plate with Lucy's and set them aside. "Sounds good. Lucy, why don't you finish coloring your picture?"

"Okay." Her daughter pulled the coloring supplies over to pick up where she'd left off. Grady worked the laptop computer, which left Lauren with nothing to do.

She sipped her coffee, staring out at the dining room that was slowly filling up with patrons. Would they make it back to Chicago in time for the Heart Ball for St. Mary's Children's Hospital? As much as she wanted to support the charity that was deeply personal to her, she wouldn't risk putting Lucy in harm's way to attend.

No matter how much she'd been looking forward to seeing Grady in a tux.

Enough. She leaned over to watch Lucy. Her daughter was intently coloring the entire paper placemat Dee had given them.

"Looks nice," she praised.

Lucy smiled, then set her crayon aside and held the drawing up toward Grady. "Grady, do you like my picture?"

Grady shut the computer and nodded, giving Lucy all his attention. He took the drawing from her fingers and admired it. "It's beautiful, Lucy. You did a nice job. I love all the different colors you used."

"Thanks. I colored it for you." Lucy held the drawing out for him. "It's yours. I hope you can put it up on your refrigerator."

"Wow, really? Thank you so much!" Grady gushed as if Lucy had given him something of value. "I love it. And of course I'll put it up on my refrigerator."

"I'm glad." When Lucy blushed, Lauren realized her daughter was crushing on Grady, seeing him as a father figure she could look up to and admire. It was probably something Lauren should have anticipated but hadn't. Hard to blame her daughter considering Lauren felt the same way.

They were quite the pair, mooning over a man they wouldn't have met under normal circumstances.

The worst part was that she didn't want Lucy's heart to be broken when this nightmare was over and they never saw Grady again. Just imagining Grady pulling on his leather coat and walking out of their life forever made her heart squeeze painfully in her chest.

And this, she thought wryly, *was why she shouldn't even consider dating*. She wasn't the only one who would be impacted by her decisions. Lucy would be a part of it too. And the last thing she wanted was for Lucy to suffer any more than necessary.

Bad enough that Lauren was living with the impacts of her past mistakes. No need to pile on with more.

Enough. She really needed to get a grip on her unruly emotions. She abruptly slid out of the booth and stood. "Come on, Lucy, let's go to the bathroom again before we leave." Lauren gestured for her daughter to come along.

"Aw, Mom," Lucy whined.

"Now, Lucy." Her tone was firm. "We might be in the car for a long time."

Lucy sighed, but then scooted out of the booth. Lauren urged her daughter toward the restroom, glancing briefly back over her shoulder to find Grady gazing down at Lucy's drawing with an intense expression.

Almost as if nobody had ever given him a simple gift like that before.

Lucy made things for her at school all the time. Something she'd taken for granted. Now, seeing the impact through Grady's eyes, she realized how precious these small tokens of appreciation really were.

When they returned to the table, Grady stood. "My turn. When I'm finished, I'll pay the bill, and then we'll head out."

"Sounds good." She grabbed Lucy's coat from the bench seat. "Here, put this on."

Ten minutes later, they were back outside. Grady sat behind the wheel for a minute, rubbing his hands together as the car slowly warmed up. This make and model didn't have accessories like heated seats or a heated steering wheel. Not that she was complaining. After all, they'd stolen the vehicle from someone who probably desperately needed it.

She still felt guilty about that. At least once they were able to get to the rental car agency, the stolen car should be recovered and returned to their rightful owner. To that end, she opened the glove box and searched for the registration. Finding nothing, she closed it. Surely, she'd be able to find the owner to properly reimburse him or her once this was over.

Grady glanced at Lucy, then at her. "Be prepared." His voice was low and husky. "We may attract attention when we get near the city limits."

She swallowed hard and nodded, understanding his concern that the stolen car might get flagged despite his efforts to alter the license plate. A tampering, now that she thought about it, that was completely illegal. Honestly, she was surprised they'd lasted this long without being caught and arrested.

Grady put the car in gear and slowly backed out of the parking lot. Driving around to the back, he left the restaurant, turning right toward Madison.

There was more traffic now, and she found herself craning her neck to see if there were cops nearby. Not that she could stop the officers from pulling them over if there were.

Turning to look behind them, she saw a dark car pulling out from a side street. She frowned. Were those tinted windows?

"Grady? Do you see this SUV?" The words barely left her mouth when the driver of the SUV put on a burst of speed and caught up to them.

"Get down, both of you!" Grady barked as the driver's side window slowly lowered. She saw the metal barrel of a gun just as she ducked her head.

Grady wrenched the wheel, sending her sideways against the car door. She heard metal screeching against metal as the two cars collided. The sharp report of gunfire had her praying for safety and that Grady hadn't been hurt.

Or worse.

"Mommy!" Lucy cried. "We crashed!"

"We're going to be okay." Grady's voice was calmly reassuring. "I just need you and your mom to keep your heads down."

Her daughter started to cry, which only made Lauren feel worse. Why was this happening? And how on earth did the gunmen find them?

Grady hit the gas, going as fast as possible, the car engine practically screaming in protest from the effort. She didn't know much about cars, but this one didn't have nearly as much power in the engine as her Porsche did.

Then another sharp crack of gunfire rang out. There was no sound of shattering glass, but that didn't mean much. Lauren closed her eyes and prayed that God would grant Grady the strength and ability to keep them safe.

10

———

Grady pushed the small car's engine to the limit to escape the gunmen. There was a turn up ahead that he took so fast the tires squealed in protest. Then he took another turn, hoping to shake the black SUV loose for good. The driver hadn't anticipated he'd sideswipe him, and the last glimpse of the SUV revealed the car was off on the side of the road.

The shrill sound of police sirens indicated someone had reported the gunfire. He wasn't sure he wanted the police to find them. At least, not yet. They'd have to report the incident, but not until they were closer to the rental car agency in Madison.

"Are we safe now?" Lauren asked, poking her head up. She turned to look at her daughter. "Lucy, are you okay back there?"

He glanced at Lucy in the rearview mirror. "Lucy, it's okay. You can sit up now. But we need to know if you're hurt."

"I'm not hurt." Lucy lifted her head and sniffled loudly. Her tear-streaked face ripped at his heart. This guy should not have been able to find them, especially since they were in a stolen car.

He forced a reassuring smile, despite the near miss. "We're safe, Lucy. I'm sorry you were scared, but we're safe now."

Lucy's wide eyes clung to his in the mirror. "Is the car broken?"

"Nope, it still works." He hadn't heard the metallic strike of a bullet, but he knew there was damage to the entire passenger side of the car from his ramming into the SUV. He scanned their surroundings, looking for any sign of the police. Seeing flashing red and blue lights up ahead, he turned into a neighborhood to avoid being seen.

"Where is the SUV?" Lauren asked with a frown.

"We lost them." How he'd managed to do that, he wasn't sure. Ramming into them had given him a slight advantage. "We're still a few miles from the rental agency." He shot her a concerned glance. "I'll get closer to the rental car agency, but we may need to abandon this car and walk for a while."

Lauren grimaced but nodded. "Whatever you think is best."

He made his way through the neighborhood homes, then got back onto a main thoroughfare. After a mile, though, he saw another pair of police cars. Maybe whoever had reported the incident had mentioned the make and model of their car. He found another neighborhood and turned. Then he stopped to park on a dead-end street.

"We'll walk from here." He reached down for the laptop. "You carry the computer. I'll carry Lucy."

"She can walk," Lauren protested.

"Maybe for a while, but I'll carry her until we're back out on the road." He slid out from behind the wheel and opened the back. "Ready, Lucy?"

The little girl nodded and allowed him to hike her up into his arms. She wasn't heavy, and his heart melted a bit when she wrapped her arms around his neck and rested her head on his shoulder.

He turned away from the stolen car and cut a path through the dead end to reach the road on the other side. Lauren followed in his wake. Grady knew they were only a mile or so from the car rental. He'd feel better once they were in a new vehicle, but it still bothered him that the black SUV had found them.

Had they been seen leaving the outlet mall parking lot? Or had the occupants of the black SUV gotten a police scanner and heard about the stolen car?

Or was someone in law enforcement involved? That seemed a stretch, as it wasn't as if the police had found them. No, the more he thought about it, the more he believed the gunmen had a police scanner. But knowing the make and model of car they'd taken didn't account for how they were found outside of Wild Prairie.

It was disheartening that these gunmen kept getting so close. If he hadn't reacted as quickly as he had, the guy may have succeeded in killing him or Lauren.

Was Lucy still the ultimate target? It was hard to imagine the goal was still to grab Lucy, yet the video of Ariel's abduction indicated the kidnapping threat was real.

And very dangerous.

"I can walk now," Lucy said after a few minutes.

"Okay." He bent to set her down. "But if you get too tired, let me know and I'll carry you again."

Lucy nodded and took a position between him and Lauren. She glanced up at her mom. "Can we make another snowman?"

"Maybe later." Lauren glanced at him. "Do you have an idea of where we should stay?"

He shrugged. "Something like the cabin rentals we used. I liked being away from the city. I'll search for a place once we get the rental car."

"That works," Lauren agreed.

A police cruiser rolled past, and Grady could tell the cop behind the wheel was watching them. Maybe because people didn't normally walk the streets in February when it was cold. They weren't breaking the law, though, so he hoped the officer wouldn't pull over to ask them a bunch of questions.

His driver's license was from Cody, Wyoming. Lauren's was from Chicago. The minute he knew they were walking to a rental car agency, the cop would be able to put two and two together to come up with the fact that they'd stolen the car.

Grady silently prayed the cop would keep going as they made their way down the street. The officer may have tracked them in his rearview mirror, but he didn't stop or turn around to talk to them.

When the sign for the rental car agency came into view, he relaxed his tense muscles. They'd made it. He held the door for Lauren and Lucy as a rush of warm air greeted them.

"Wait here," he said to Lauren. He went to the counter and gave the clerk the information Rex had used to rent the car.

Ten minutes later, he had the keys in hand and was headed back outside to get their dark metallic-gray SUV. As requested, there was a booster seat in the back for Lucy.

"This is nice," Lauren said, when they were once again back on the road. Grady headed north, away from the city.

"You should stop near a coffee shop so we can use the internet to find another place to stay."

"Good idea." He wanted to leave the city as soon as possible, but having a destination in mind would help. Seeing a well-known coffee shop up ahead, he pulled into the parking lot and parked.

Lauren opened the laptop and connected to the free internet. After a few minutes of searching, she turned the computer so he could see the screen. "How about this place? It's just like the cabin rental."

He scanned the information on the screen. "Looks like they have openings and are only about an hour away. I need to stop at a bank first, then we'll head out."

"A bank?" She frowned. "I thought we were staying off the radar. I can pull money out of my account if needed."

"I don't want to use your name in an ATM transaction." It was bad enough he was going to use his own. Whoever was behind these attacks likely knew his name by now. And that was the first step to being able to track his movements. Yet it couldn't be helped. They needed cash, and obtaining the funds from a bank here in the city was their best option.

The bank wasn't far, and he had Lauren and Lucy wait in the car while he withdrew the money. Having two thousand in cash made him feel better. Although he also knew they'd need to stop at a grocery store again to buy more food.

Lauren put a kibosh on buying more Captain Jack's pizza. Instead, they settled on soup and sandwiches for lunch and dinner.

He really wanted to talk to Griff, then depending on what he learned from that conversation, he'd reach out to Agent Braun. He empathized with Lauren's frustration over the lack of progress on the case. He didn't understand why it was taking so long for the FBI to find kidnappers. It occurred to him that if Braun had arranged to interview Eric Howington and Karla Dalton back in Chicago, then they couldn't be riding in an SUV here in Madison, firing a gun at them.

"Turn left here," Lauren said, interrupting his thoughts. "The next highway will take us where we want to go."

"Okay." He headed north to get out of the city. The cops that had been around earlier seemed to have dispersed. Maybe they'd already found their abandoned stolen car.

The trip didn't take long, but he realized this particular section of the state was composed of several acres of farmland. They passed one smaller farm, but the next one was huge. Not only were there big stretches of open land, but the farm had a huge outbuilding and barn to go along with the white farmhouse.

"I haven't seen large farms like this before," Lauren murmured as they drove past. "I guess living in the city makes it easy to forget that someone has to grow and raise the livestock to provide the food we eat."

"Where are the cows?" Lucy asked.

"They might be in the barn since it's cold outside." He wasn't an expert on farming either. The Sullivan K9 Search and Rescue Ranch had horses and dogs, lots of dogs, but they didn't run cattle or raise chickens. When they passed the farm, he caught a glimpse of a cluster of cattle huddled behind the barn. "There they are, seeking shelter from the wind."

"I see them!" Lucy looked excited.

He nodded, turning at the next intersection. The cabin rentals Lauren had found weren't far. As he followed the signs leading them to Calvin's Cabins, he was surprised to see there was a small patch of woods on one side of the cabin rentals, while the open farmland stretched beyond the other.

Having woods on all sides had been nice, and for a moment, he debated whether to stay here or head someplace else. The cabins were somewhat secluded, so he decided to just stay there. At least for the next twenty-four hours.

This time he was given cabin number nine, which was farthest from the two-story home that doubled as a lobby. The guy behind the desk looked to be almost eighty, with white hair, white beard, and a large belly that protruded over his belt. Thankfully, the elderly owner was more than happy to take cash.

"Just one night?" The guy looked disappointed. "Not the whole weekend?"

"We might stay another night. I should know more by tomorrow morning." Grady smiled and gave the guy an extra twenty. "Thanks again."

"Anytime." The twenty along with the other two hundred in cash disappeared into his pocket.

Once they were settled inside the cabin, he called Griff but was forced to leave a message. Same thing when he called FBI Agent Braun.

"Should I start making calls?" Lauren asked with a frown. "They should be getting back to us about what they'd found."

"Not yet." He sat at the table and opened the computer. He still hadn't finished going through the social media posts of Nelson's frat brothers. "Let's do a little more work first."

She sighed and glanced over at Lucy who was watching television. "I don't love all this screen time, and I really hate knowing she's missing school."

"I understand." He hoped the case would be solved by

Monday. "There's one name I ran into last night on Archer's social media account. A guy by the name of Curtis Handover." He glanced at her. "Does that sound familiar?"

"Nope." She sat in the chair beside him. "Why did he catch your eye?"

"Because he said something about Bobby Morton's death." He scrolled through the site to find the comment. "Something that indicated he was a good friend of Bobby's."

"Even so, that doesn't mean he'd try to kidnap Lucy." Lauren frowned. "Unless you think Nelson is a friend of his too?"

"No, it sounded as if Curtis wasn't happy with your ex." He found the comment and turned the screen so she could read it for herself. "See this? He wrote: 'Bobby shouldn't have died and being sent to prison isn't enough of a punishment.'"

"Yeah, I see that. But I still don't think that means he'd kidnap Nelson's daughter as payback."

He shrugged. "Maybe this Curtis guy is Bobby's cousin or something, since they have different last names."

After entering the new name in the search engine, he found Curtis Handover's social media page. The second picture was one that featured Curtis and Bobby standing next to each other, grinning at the camera. The caption simply said, "my brother."

"His brother?" Lauren frowned. "You mean he has another relative other than Randy?"

"Different last name could mean he's a half brother or even a stepbrother." He did a quick criminal background check on Curtis Handover. The guy's record was clean. Going back to social media, he dug further until he found a post where the two men were standing with their respective mothers. The post was captioned, "different moms with the same love."

"They share a father." He turned to stare at Lauren. "It looks to me like Curtis blames Nelson for his half brother's death."

"A half brother in addition to a first cousin," Lauren echoed in a low voice. "Why didn't any of the cops or the FBI mention Curtis? Did they even bother to dig into Bobby's family to look for suspects?"

"I don't know." He shared her concern. "Hopefully, we'll know more when either Griff or David Braun calls me back."

She reached over to grasp his hand. "Do you think we're getting close to uncovering the truth?"

He smiled reassuringly to show his faith in the system, despite how it was his digging that had unearthed another possible suspect. "Yeah, I'm sure this nightmare will be over very soon."

She nodded, but her troubled gaze remained on the image of Curtis and Bobby hugging their respective mothers.

A non-traditional family that had been torn apart by her ex-husband's carless decision to drive while under the influence.

THERE WAS no reason to feel guilty over Bobby's tragic death, but logic didn't seem to matter. Lauren wasn't responsible for the way Nelson had crashed while driving drunk. And her daughter certainly didn't deserve to pay the price, if this was about revenge.

She rose and paced the length of the cabin, feeling rest-less. The police should have known about Bobby's half brother as well as his cousin. They should have already interviewed them and either cleared them or kept them as a suspect.

And the gunmen should not be here in Wisconsin, finding them despite their attempts to stay off-grid.

She stared blindly through the narrow opening between the trees at the large farm located west of the cabin. They'd been running from danger for what seemed like forever, with no end in sight. She wanted to scream in frustration but did her best to tamp down her anger.

When Grady's phone rang, she spun from the window like it was a gunshot. Then she crossed over to be included in the conversation.

"Hi, Griff, I'm putting you on speaker," Grady said. "Lauren is here. You need to know what's been going on since we last spoke."

"I'm getting the impression you don't like the Chicago FBI," Griff drawled. "Do I need to fly across the country to help you?"

"No, but you're right about the Chicago FBI," Grady agreed. "I feel like they're two steps behind us when it should be the other way around."

"Okay, what happened?" Griff asked.

She listened as Grady filled him in. At some level, she found it difficult to believe this was really happening to her and Lucy. That someone had kidnapped Ariel by mistake and was determined to get it right the second time around.

Even if that meant killing anyone who got in the way.

"How do you keep getting found?" Griff asked, clearly perplexed.

"Maybe the Chicago FBI?" Grady drawled. When she

frowned, he shrugged, and added, "It could be that the gunmen have a police scanner and figured out we stole the car. But how they found us on our way to picking up the rental car is a mystery."

There was a muffled voice in the background, then Griff asked, "Dom wants to know if you've been on the internet?"

"Yes, we have been using the internet, but why does that matter?" Grady asked. "I don't see how using the free cabin rental internet or the breakfast restaurant internet or any others would lead these guys to us."

"You'd be surprised by what a computer geek can do as far as tracking internet usage," Griff said. "Dom thinks you should stay off the internet from here on out."

Lauren reached over to disconnect the laptop from the internet, then powered it down. While she didn't understand how using the access drew the bad guys to their location, she wasn't willing to take the chance.

"Do you think we need to move to a new place?" Grady's brow was furrowed with concern. "Because we can."

"How long have you been there?" Griff asked.

"About an hour," Grady admitted. "And we've been online the entire time."

"Yes, Dom says you need to get out of there. I don't understand all the geek speak, but he's worried that's how you're being tracked."

"Okay, we'll head out right away." Grady's expression was grim. "But I need you to investigate a guy by the name of Curtis Handover; he's Bobby Morton's half brother. We think he could be working with Bobby's first cousin, Randy Morton."

"You think they're seeking revenge?" Griff sounded skeptical.

"We don't know." Grady paused, then added, "We

haven't found anything on Randy, but Curtis Handover posted something on social media that leads me to believe he is upset with Nelson Derringer about his half brother's death."

"Okay, I can see why you'd want both of them checked out," Griff agreed. "The local police didn't mention them?"

"Nope. And while I don't know why Curtis Handover, Randy Morton, or anyone else for that matter would try to kidnap Lucy now, it certainly does feel like revenge is the driving motivation behind this. That and money," he added.

Lauren believed the reverse was true. That the goal was more about the money, with the revenge angle being an added bonus.

"I think you can trust Agent Braun," Griff was saying. "I'll reach out to him while you get Lauren and her daughter someplace safe."

"Understood. We'll talk later." Grady disconnected from the line. "I feel bad I didn't consider they could track us via the internet."

"It's okay." She had never thought of it either. She stood and headed into the living room. "Get your coat, Lucy. We need to go for anther ride."

"No, I'm watching my show," Lucy said without tearing her gaze from the television. One of the many reasons why Lauren didn't like allowing so much screen time.

"Now, Lucy." Grady's stern tone caught her daughter's attention. Lucy frowned at Grady, then scrambled off the sofa to reach for her coat. Lauren swallowed her annoyance at how her daughter listened to Grady better than to her, her own mother.

"Let me grab the groceries." Lauren moved into the kitchen. "I don't want to waste them."

"Yeah, I'll help." Grady quickly filled one of the grocery bags they'd just emptied. "We'll leave the computer behind."

Packing their things didn't take long. Lauren thought they would make it out of there when she saw a dark car driving up to the log cabin. She grabbed Grady's arm, squeezing tightly. "I think they're here."

"I see them." He eyed the rental, but the only way out of the cabin would take them past the black SUV with tinted windows. "Follow me, we're going around back on foot."

On foot? She wanted to argue, but there wasn't time to waste. She turned toward Lucy, and whispered, "Come this way."

Lucy's eyes widened in fear, but she nodded and followed her lead. Leaving everything behind, they went back inside the cabin, then headed out the back door. The small woods didn't extend very far, and beyond them, there was nothing but open farmer's fields.

She tripped over a tree root, her mind spinning. If they kept going, the bad guys would see them! Unless they could somehow get to the outbuildings in time.

Sending up a silent prayer, she quickened her pace. When Lucy dragged behind, Grady abruptly turned and picked her daughter up into his arms. He lengthened his stride, heading between the trees and into the farmer's field.

The snow wasn't as deep as she anticipated, yet it still felt as if they were moving at a snail's pace. She kept glancing over her shoulder, expecting to see the black SUV coming straight toward them. The car might just make it across the rutted farmer's field.

She set her jaw and jogged to keep up with Grady. If he could make good time carrying Lucy, then she'd find a way to keep up as well.

After what seemed like eons, they reached the first outbuilding. Grady set Lucy on her feet, then shoved the massive door aside. She had to blink her eyes to adjust to the dim interior of what appeared to be an equipment storage shed.

Grady headed for an old beat-up truck. She was about to follow when she saw the distinct wing of a small airplane.

The farmer owned a small plane? She headed toward the bird, wondering if it was usable. Grady was already poking around under the truck's hood.

"This is in bad shape," he said, more to himself than to her. "We might want to just head up to the house to see if anyone inside can call for help."

"Hang on." She opened the door of the plane that she assumed was used as a crop duster. Either to spread fertilizer or to kill pests, she wasn't entirely sure. She climbed up and examined the cockpit.

"Grady? Someone is coming," Lucy said, her voice panicked.

"I see the black SUV, Lucy. Stay back from the door." Grady's voice sounded strained. "Lauren, we need to get up to the farmhouse right away."

"The men in the car are armed." She couldn't stand the thought of the farmer and his family being hurt in the scuffle. Especially since they were far enough out of town that it would take the police a long time to get there. "We can take the plane."

"I hate to break it to you, but the army didn't teach me how to fly a plane," Grady said. "They taught me to shoot a gun."

"I have a pilot's license." She started the motor and was impressed the engine started right up. Despite the condition of the truck, the farmer obviously kept the plane in good repair. This was their best chance to escape. She didn't like taking something that didn't belong to her, but she wasn't about to let that stop her from saving her daughter.

If this worked, they'd be long gone before the gunmen could find them again.

11

———————

Lauren had a pilot's license? Grady was stunned. He vaguely remembered her saying something about her father having a plane when they were getting out of Chicago, but he hadn't expected this.

There wasn't time to ask questions, though. He lifted Lucy into the plane, then ran forward to open the massive garage door so they could head outside. His heart thumped painfully in his chest as he saw the black SUV in the distance rounding the curve in the road to head toward the farmhouse.

They needed to get out of there, and fast! He turned and sprinted back to the plane, vaulting inside. "Go! They're coming our way!" he shouted above the roar of the plane engines.

Lauren gave a terse nod and moved the plane's yoke to propel them forward. Grady pulled his weapon, only to realize the plane wasn't like a car where you could roll down the window to shoot. He held his breath as the small plane picked up speed. A surge of doubt hit hard. Would this work? Would the plane get airborne?

To her credit, Lauren seemed to know what she was doing. As she worked the controls, he told himself to trust her skills. Honestly, he was more worried the plane engine might fail or that they wouldn't have enough fuel to escape. Not that they had much of a choice but to follow through with this plan. They were so far outside of the city that calling 911 for help was useless. There was no way the police would get there in time.

The wide driveway stretching out before them likely doubled as a runway, but it was also the same path the black SUV was using to close in on them. Grady gripped his weapon tightly, bracing himself for the occupants of the car to start firing at them. He was surprised they hadn't tried to do that already, but they were still far enough apart that a handgun wouldn't have the accuracy they needed.

A fact that worked against him, too, even if he could shoot at the SUV from the plane. Somehow, he didn't think opening the door would be a smart move. His experience in the army was with choppers that could fly with the doors open. He didn't know much about small planes.

His mouth went dry as he watched through the windshield as Lauren and the black SUV played a game of chicken. It was like something out of a movie. Lauren didn't let up on the plane controls, continuing to push forward despite the black SUV barreling toward them. The driver of the SUV appeared to be doing the same. Grady had to resist the urge to close his eyes when the gap between the plane and the car closed dramatically.

Then Lauren pulled back on the yoke, lifting the small plane into the air. Pressing his face to the side window, he watched as the black SUV jerked to a stop, the driver's side door and the passenger-side doors opening as the two occupants bailed from the vehicle.

"Higher," he shouted, anticipating their attempt to shoot them down. "You need to get us higher!"

She nodded, never taking her gaze from the control panel. The nose of the plane continued to climb to the point he could see they were rising above the treetops. As an escape plan, this wasn't too bad.

Until he heard the sharp report of gunfire as the two men below unleashed their weapons. He twisted in his seat, trying to see them. Lauren must have had nerves of steel because she didn't so much as flinch.

She flipped a switch, and he was surprised to see chemicals dropping down to the ground beneath them. Whatever pesticide or fertilizer that had been stored in the cargo section of the plane was now covering the gunman and the SUV.

"Good job," he shouted, grinning widely.

She barely looked at him as she banked the plane into a wide curve, changing their course. The maneuver gave him a better view of the two gunmen below. They were too small for him to see any details to provide an accurate description. At this distance, he couldn't even say for sure they were both men. That was the impression he had from watching how they'd moved out of the car and pointed their weapons up toward the. Yet having served with female soldiers, he couldn't afford to make any assumptions. When the chemicals flowed down from the plane, the two gunmen stopped firing and ducked back into the car.

"We're clear," he shouted. Then, for the first time, he turned to check on Lucy. He found the little girl huddled behind Lauren's pilot seat. Lucy had her palms pressed tightly to her ears to muffle the noise. Under different circumstances, they'd have had headphones with an intercom to enable them to communicate. Obviously, that hadn't been at the top of the priority list as they escaped the farm. Lauren had done her best under the circumstances. He reached out his hand to touch the young girl's arm. "Lucy, are you okay?"

Her blue eyes clung to his. She nodded jerkily, but he could tell she was scared to death. This was probably the first time Lucy had been in a small plane like this with her mother behind the controls. He smiled reassuringly.

"Your mom is amazing," he said loudly. "She's getting us to safety."

Lucy nodded again, but this time her mouth tipped up in a slight smile as if agreeing with him about her mom being amazing. He patted her arm, then turned toward Lauren. "How far can you take us?"

Lauren glanced at him, then back at the control panel. "This is a crop duster, so I'm not entirely sure. I expect to find a place to land somewhere close to Madison."

"Sounds good." He swallowed hard, not entirely thrilled to be heading back to Madison, considering they'd only left the city less than a few hours ago. He suspected the drivers of the SUV would anticipate the city of Madison would be their likely destination as it was the closest airport. No doubt a crop duster like this couldn't get them all the way back to Illinois. The good news was that he, Lauren, and Lucy were traveling much faster than a car could go. They would get to the city first.

Unfortunately, he anticipated the black SUV with the tinted windows wouldn't be too far behind.

Now that the threat of danger was over at least for the moment, Grady leaned forward to inspect the instrument panel. He noticed Lauren kept the plane at an altitude of about one thousand feet above sea level, making him wonder if that was the maximum height a plane like this could go. He assumed most crop-duster planes flew at much lower altitudes than other small planes.

She flipped another switch, and this time, a radio crackled to life. He listened as Lauren explained they were coming in for an unexpected landing. The voice on the other end of the radio sounded annoyed, demanding to know the plane's registration numbers and berating her for not submitting a flight plan.

He would have jumped in, but Lauren had the situation under control. Ignoring the questions, she repeated her position that they were entering the Madison county airspace for an unexpected landing in a calm tone. When the guy repeated his grievances over her actions, she flipped the switch, killing the radio connection.

Grady saw the airport off to the starboard side of their plane. The Madison airport was much bigger than he'd expected. There was one jumbo jet coming in for a landing while others were in line to take off. Their crop duster could easily get in the way of the other planes if they weren't careful. He glanced nervously at Lauren, hoping she knew how and, more importantly, *where* to land this thing.

He needn't have worried. Lauren gave the main airport a wide berth, coming in low on the far side of the airport, far away from where the big jets were coming and going. This area of the airfield had individual hangar buildings, several with open doors revealing small planes parked inside. The landing strips were shorter here, too, keeping the much smaller planes out of the main thoroughfare. He stared down at one plane that was bigger than their crop duster and the four people standing outside who were clearly waiting to climb aboard.

"We're going to crash," Lucy cried.

"No, don't worry, we won't crash." The words had barely

left his mouth when Lauren landed the plane with a light bounce, then slowed to a stop. Grady was impressed with her skill. She'd barely released her grip on the yoke when he leaned over to wrap his arms around her. "That was amazing!"

"Thanks." She blushed, hugging him back. "I am glad that farmer keeps his plane in top-notch condition. This flight could have gone very differently if he hadn't." She blew out a breath, then turned toward her daughter. "Did you like your first small plane ride, Lucy?"

"Yes, but it was too loud." Lucy climbed into the narrow space between the seats, her earlier fear of crashing seemingly abated. "Are we going to take another plane ride to go home now?"

Home. The word stabbed deep into Grady's heart. He wanted nothing more than to assure the little girl that she would be safe. That nobody would grab her, the way the kidnapper had taken Ariel.

But he couldn't. This recent incident had been another close call. He felt awful knowing that his connecting to the internet had led the gunman straight to their cabin.

Not anymore, he thought darkly. He was sick and tired of the gunmen finding them.

"Sit tight while I call Rex." He pulled out his phone. "I'm sure he can arrange for us to get a ride out of here."

Lauren nodded, holding Lucy close as he connected with Rex.

"What did you say?" his boss demanded. "Lauren flew you out of harm's way in a crop duster?"

"That's right." He smiled reassuringly as Lauren arched a brow. "She's an amazing pilot, and we were able to get back to Madison safely. I need you to arrange for another rental car since we had to leave the other one behind."

His boss sighed loudly. "Okay, but the way you're driving our expenses through the roof is eating into our profit margin."

A flash of anger hit hard. Lauren's and Lucy's lives were at stake. He didn't care one bit about Rex Grayson's profit margin.

"Tell Rex I'll reimburse him the additional expenses," Lauren said calmly.

He shook his head, unwilling to pass that message along. What Lauren and Rex decided once the gunmen were behind bars wasn't his concern. Right now, he just wanted them to be safe. A task that was proving to be more difficult than he'd anticipated. "You can take the cost out of my fee. I don't care. Just get us another rental car." When he saw small van driving away from the private jet, he added, "We'll find a ride to the main airport terminal. There must be plenty of car rentals available there."

"I'll make the arrangements," Rex agreed. "What else can I help you with?"

"Nothing at the moment." He decided not to go into detail about how Griff's tech expert Dominic had revealed they'd been tracked by the internet. "Thanks."

"Yep. Stay safe," Rex said, before ending the call.

He pocketed his phone and nodded at Lauren and Lucy. "Ready to get out of here?"

They nodded. He climbed out first, then held out his arms for Lucy. When they were on the tarmac, a small van rolled toward them.

He moved forward first, making sure they weren't walking into a trap. When the kid behind the wheel looked barely old enough to drive, he gestured for Lauren and Lucy to hop in.

The first leg of their escape plan had worked beautifully.

Now all he needed to do was to keep them safe long enough to get out of the city before the gunmen found them again.

Lauren was glad that Grady hadn't noticed how badly her hands were shaking. It wasn't her first time flying a small plane; she wasn't lying about having a pilot's license. But taking a crop duster from a farmer, not knowing what sort of maintenance had been done on the engine, had been a gamble. Worse, because Lucy and Grady were with her. It would have been her fault if they'd crashed.

Thankfully, the farmer had kept his plane in good repair. She made a mental note of the plane's tail number, something she hadn't noticed before they'd jumped in to get away from the black SUV, so she could repay the owner and thank him for the role he'd played in keeping her daughter safe.

The van driver dropped them off near a private terminal. From there, they walked to the main airport. Grady took the lead in heading to the rental car agency. She'd felt bad hearing Rex's comment about the expenses. For one thing, it certainly wasn't their fault these guys were so determined to track them down.

Second, she would gladly pay for the extra expense. Why Grady hadn't passed her comment along was puzzling. There was no reason for him to use his own money to pay the extra expense. Both men had to know there was nothing more important to her than keeping Lucy safe.

"I wish we could go home," Lucy whispered.

"I know, sweetie. Me too." She wrapped her arm around Lucy's shoulders as Grady signed the paperwork on their rental. "Hopefully soon."

Lucy leaned against her. "I love you, Mom."

"I love you too." She pressed a kiss on Lucy's head. Her daughter had been through a lot over the past few hours. And the day was far from over.

At this rate, they'd never make it back to Chicago in time for St. Mary's Valentine's Day charity ball.

"Ready to go?" Grady came away from the rental car counter with a key fob in his hand. "The car is ready."

"Yes." She hugged Lucy again, then straightened. "Lucy, stay between us, okay?"

Lucy clung to her hand as they walked back outside. The cold wind blew into their faces, making her shiver. Grady scanned their surroundings as they crossed the road to the rental car parking lot. His intense gaze made her realize he was making sure the black SUV with tinted windows wasn't waiting for them.

The thought of the gunmen returning to finish the job made her shiver. Was kidnapping Lucy even their main goal anymore? It didn't seem to be. Not after the two gunmen had gotten out of the car to shoot at the plane as they flew overhead, which indicated that their intent was to kill them all in one fell swoop.

Yet where on earth was the financial gain in killing them? Could Nelson have taken out some sort of life insurance policy on her? Even if he had, that wouldn't explain Ariel's kidnapping.

Her nerves were back on edge as Grady found the rental car, a light-gray Jeep SUV. He frowned, and she wondered if he'd preferred the dark-colored vehicle they'd gotten before. He didn't say anything, though, just opened the doors for her and Lucy.

Like last time, there was a child booster seat in the back.

Rex had remembered to request one, and she was grateful to have the additional layer of protection.

"Oh goody, this booster seat is just like mine at home," Lucy said as she climbed in.

"Glad you approve," Grady drawled with a wry smile.

Lauren slid into the passenger seat as Grady waited for Lucy to get buckled in. Then he closed the door and slid in behind the wheel. Moments later, they were out on the road, heading away from the airport. She stared at the cars around them, seeing way too many black SUVs for her peace of mind.

"We should be fine," Grady said in a low tone, obviously keying in on her stress levels. "We lost a little time driving from the landing strip, but not much."

"I'm sure you're right." She tried to shake off the feeling of despair. Maybe it was the adrenaline crash after the escaping the farm. Thankfully, none of the black SUVs passing them by had tinted windows. "Where are we going this time?"

"South." Grady nodded toward the highway. "I think we should make our way back toward Illinois. Not crossing the state line but finding a place to stay that is closer to the border."

"Really?" She was surprised by his decision. "Why?"

He sighed and shrugged. "I'm hoping the gunmen won't be searching for us there. Avoiding the tollway should keep us safely off their radar."

"Good." She rolled her shoulders in an effort to relax. "Staying incognito would be very good."

"What does incognito mean?" Lucy asked.

"It means keeping our identity a surprise." She turned to smile at her daughter. "Don't worry, we're safe now."

"Okay." Lucy seemed to take her statement at face value,

which was a little surprising because every time they'd thought they were safe, the gunmen had managed to find them.

They drove in silence for several minutes. Lauren saw the sign indicating they were thirty miles from Lake Geneva. The town sounded familiar, and she'd heard several people from Chicago liked to stay there. That alone would have been a reason to stay away.

Rather than avoiding the city, Grady headed straight toward it. As they grew closer, she eyed him curiously. "I thought you didn't want to go to touristy places?"

He grimaced. "To be honest, I'm hoping the same theory applies. That the gunmen will assume we're heading north or east avoiding places like this. Besides, I don't plan to stay in the area for long. If we need to find another place to spend the night, we'll look for something else."

She assumed that was because hotels normally had rules that prevented people from paying in cash.

"I'm hungry," Lucy said from the back seat. "Did we miss lunch?"

"Yeah, we did." She reached over to touch Grady's arm. "What do you think? Can we afford to stop for lunch in Lake Geneva?"

"Sure thing. They have plenty of restaurants," Grady said. "And that will give us time to connect with David Braun too. He should have something to tell us by now."

She wasn't sure about that. It seemed to her as if the FBI was moving in slow motion. The local police too.

They rode in silence for several minutes. Grady slowed his speed as they approached the resort town. The lake itself was pretty, even in the cold and snowy conditions. Huge mansions lined the lakeshore as far as the eye could see. Lauren had never personally been to Lake Geneva, but the town felt very familiar. It was obvious the high-end jewelry, clothing, and art shops catered to the wealthy.

About as different from the cabin rentals Grady had used as the sun from the moon. She imagined the hotels here cost five times what he'd spent on the cabin.

Strangely, she discovered she liked staying at the cabin better. They were clean, low key, and isolated from the rest of the world.

From what she could tell, the city of Lake Geneva didn't offer cabin rentals as an option. Unless there were some located outside the city, far away from the downtown area.

"There's a restaurant up ahead that appears to be open." Grady frowned as he slowly drove through the picturesque town. "I'm surprised some of them are closed considering it's a Friday."

"It's the off season," she said with a shrug. "There isn't much to do on a frozen lake."

"Can we build another snowman?" Lucy asked.

"Maybe later." She knew their plans for the rest of the day were up in the air. Especially since this stop had been a spur of the moment decision. "Looks like there's a small parking lot over there."

Grady pulled in and killed the engine. He pushed out of the SUV, then opened the back door so Lucy could get out.

There weren't many cars in the lot, but she tensed when she noticed one was a black SUV. Lauren stared at it as they walked past, half expecting a gunman to pop out from the driver's seat. When she caught a glimpse of a small stuffed animal lying in the back seat, she released her pent-up breath.

A family vehicle. Not the bad guys.

She gave herself a mental shake. It was time to stop imagining there were gunmen hiding around every corner.

There was no possible way the black SUV could find them there."

The restaurant sported a nautical theme, which didn't necessarily go along with the shocking red Valentine's Day decorations. Grady asked for a booth, and they were led to a table with a nice view of the lake.

"Can I have chicken bites?" Lucy asked once they were settled on the bench seat across from Grady.

Her first instinct was to refuse. The last thing her daughter needed was more processed food. But then she remembered how scared Lucy had been during their unplanned plane escape, not to mention the previous shooting incidents. One more day of eating whatever she wanted wouldn't hurt. Lauren nodded. "Yes, if that's an option on the menu."

"Looks like they have chicken strips, which is practically the same thing." Grady was already scanning his menu. "We'll put our order in first, then I'll reach out to Agent Braun."

Their server took their drink orders first. She and Grady went with coffee, while Lucy had another glass of chocolate milk. Once their drinks arrived, she put in a request for Lucy's chicken strips, along with a grilled chicken wrap. Grady, of course, went for the double-decker cheeseburger.

Once they were alone, Grady reached for his phone. "I hope Braun answers this time," he groused.

He made the call, then groaned when Braun's voice mail kicked in. "Braun, it's Grady and Lauren. Call us back as soon as possible." He ended the call. "I don't know what he's doing."

She sat back in the booth, trying to give the FBI agent the benefit of doubt. "Maybe he's handling the interviews."

Grady looked pointedly at his watch. "It's noon. He's had all morning to do them."

She glanced at Lucy who was blowing bubbles into her chocolate milk. "You're assuming he's found them in the first place. They could be here driving around in a black SUV."

"Maybe." He scrubbed his hands over his face. "We need answers."

No argument there. She was about to take Lucy to the bathroom when his phone rang. Grady answered, putting the call on speaker. "Agent Braun?"

"Yeah, I got your message. Things have been happening fast around here."

Lauren had to bite her lip to keep from snapping at him. He thought things were happening in Chicago? They'd jumped into a stolen crop-duster plane to escape!

"Fill us in," Grady said.

"I just interviewed Eric Howington," Braun said. She and Grady exchanged glances. There hadn't been enough time for the black SUV to get from Madison to Chicago, which meant Howington wasn't their guy. "He's clear, has an ironclad alibi for the first abduction and for the time of the shooting of your penthouse apartment."

"Okay, good to know we can cross him off our list," Grady said. "What else?"

"I've left several messages for Karla Dalton, but she hasn't returned my calls. You should know that Randy Morton, Bobby's first cousin, is dead. He died of a drug over-dose three months ago. We didn't know about Bobby Morton's half brother, Curtis Handover, so we dug into him. I discovered he's been posting threats aimed at Nelson Derringer."

Lauren straightened in her seat. "What kind of threats?"

"Threats that make it clear Nelson should watch his

back when he's released from prison. Which will happen on Monday morning."

Monday? Lauren's heart squeezed in her chest. What happened to two more months?

"Have you reached out to Handover?" Grady asked. "Do you have any idea where he is?"

"He's not at home, but he has a black Honda SUV registered in his name. I've issued a tri-statewide BOLO for him, and I am sure we'll have him in custody by the end of the day."

Lauren stared at Grady in shock. Curtis Handover was one of the shooters!

She bowed her head and silently prayed the police would find and arrest him very soon. Bringing an end to this nightmare.

12

———

Grady understood from Lauren's relieved expression that she believed Curtis Handover was their shooter. The guy did own a black SUV, so it made sense. Yet oddly, he wasn't convinced. He cleared his throat. "Agent Braun, will you let us know when you find Curtis Handover to bring him in for questioning?"

"That's the plan," Braun agreed. "I'm sure one of the police officers will spot his vehicle and grab him for us."

"Thank you," Lauren said. "Lucy and I will be so happy when this nightmare is over."

"Yes, thank you." Grady reached over to end the call. He was glad the feds planned to move fast on this new intel. But why hadn't the FBI found the connection between Curtis Handover and Bobby Morton sooner? He thought it was interesting Randy had died of a drug overdose. Addiction obviously ran in the family. But they should have known about Curtis, watching his movements shortly after Ariel's abduction.

Yet it was odd that Curtis would be so clueless as to post threatening comments on social media before setting up a kidnapping attempt. Then again, nobody claimed criminals were smart. There were prisons full of criminals who'd gotten caught because of their actions.

"I'm so glad we came south to Lake Geneva." Lauren sat back in her seat with a sigh. "It's nice to be that much closer to home."

In his mind, home wasn't a penthouse apartment, but obviously, it was to Lauren and Lucy. He smiled reassuringly. "We'll stick around here for a while until we hear back from Agent Braun."

"That's fine with me." She glanced up as their server approached with their meals. "Perfect timing."

Grady nodded and decided not to share his concerns. Lauren looked so happy he couldn't bear to wipe the smile off her face. When their server topped off their coffee and left, he reached across the table for Lauren's hand.

"I'd like to say grace."

"Oh, are we praying again?" Lucy asked.

He nodded and took her hand too. "Yes. Remember what I said earlier?" He bowed his head. "Dear Lord Jesus, we thank You for this food we are blessed to eat. We also ask that You continue to keep us safe in Your care. Amen."

"Amen," Lucy said.

"Amen," Lauren echoed. Then she smiled. "Thanks to you, Grady, I've been praying a lot since this started. I'd like to find a church to attend once we get home."

He nodded, humbled by her words. He was glad to have been a part of her faith journey. He wasn't so sure there were churches in the downtown area of Chicago, though. That seemed price prohibitive considering the real estate market was sky high in urban cities. "I can help you find something close by if you like."

"That would be nice." Lauren watched ruefully as Lucy

dug into her chicken tenders. "I'm going to have a hard time convincing her to eat healthy once this is over."

He grimaced, stung by a stab of guilt. "Sorry."

She waved that off. "I know I probably went a little overboard because of Lucy's surgery, but I was so scared."

"I know." He figured his double-decker cheeseburger was off-limits as well. "To be honest, I think it's good that you encourage Lucy to eat healthy and expose her to different foods. More parents should do that."

"Thank you." She dug in to her chicken wrap.

Grady took a bite of his cheeseburger and was glad he'd ordered it. The burger was juicy and delicious. He felt like he'd burned thousands of calories since he'd been tasked to protect Lauren and her daughter.

For their sake, he hoped Curtis Handover was the kidnapper/shooter and that he'd be off the street soon. But that didn't stop him from noticing every single black SUV that passed by the restaurant outside. None had tinted windows, so he tried not to overreact.

Lauren must have noticed, though, because she frowned. "I'm sure we're safe here."

He shrugged. "I plan to stay alert just in case."

"Okay." She smiled at Lucy who was clearly enjoying her chicken strips. "I can't wait to get back home. I need to reimburse the owner of the car and the crop-duster plane, not just for the items but for their time and the inconvenience we've caused. I know they won't be thrilled, but I hope that letting them know the only reason we took their things was to stay safe will take the sting out of our actions."

The owner of the car might still be upset, but he figured the farmer who owned the crop duster wouldn't mind too much. It's not as if he needed to use the plane in the winter. "I'm sure they'll be happy with whatever you give them."

"I hope so." She turned and shook her head at Lucy. "No more blowing bubbles in your chocolate milk, you're spilling on the table."

"Aw, Mom." Lucy had a chocolate milk mustache. "I'm just having fun."

Grady was about to say something about how she should listen to her mother, but then he caught himself. He wasn't Lucy's father. He needed to stay out of it.

They ate in silence for a few minutes. When they finished, Lauren and Lucy made another stop in the restroom. He paid the tab, then glanced outside just as another black SUV rolled down the street. The angle of the sun was such that he couldn't tell if the windows were tinted.

He strode quickly to the window to get a better look at the license plate. His pulse kicked up when he recognized the Illinois plate, but he only caught the first three letters, which were APW. He pulled out his phone and called Agent Braun. Once again, the call went straight to his voice mail.

Did the fed ever answer his phone? Irritated, Grady left a terse message. "It's McFarland. I need to know the license plate of Curtis Handover's SUV. Call me back."

Maybe he was overreacting, but he decided they shouldn't head outside anytime soon. At least, not until he knew what they were looking for. Feeling restless, he moved toward a rack of brochures that listed various tourist activities taking place in the area. There was one for a magic show at a nearby theater.

Something like that would keep Lucy preoccupied for a while. He noticed there was an afternoon matinee session in about an hour, along with one in the evening. He pocketed the brochure and turned as Lauren and Lucy emerged from the restrooms.

His phone rang before he could tell them about the magic show. Seeing Agent Braun's number on the screen, he quickly answered. "Braun? Do you have the plate number?"

"I do, it's EFY1008." There was a brief pause, then Braun asked, "Why are you asking?"

It wasn't a match to the car he'd seen, but Grady wasn't sure if that was a good thing or a bad one. What if Curtis Handover wasn't their guy and the SUV outside did belong to the gunmen? His paranoia was getting difficult to control, but he did his best to tamp it down. "I want to watch for it. Unless you have him in custody already?"

"Not yet." Now Agent Braun sounded testy. "It's barely a half hour since we last talked, McFarland. Tell Ms. Chandler there's no need to start making calls to her political friends. We're expanding our reach to find him."

"Have you tried the tollway?" Grady asked. "We know for sure he crossed the state line into Wisconsin."

"Yes, we're working on that. I have our tech guy searching for the vehicle now." Braun's tone softened. "Trust me, we'll find him."

He didn't bother to point out that he didn't trust anyone except his boss and the Sullivan family. "Okay, thanks." He lowered the phone and quickly filled Lauren in on the license plate information, without mentioning the black SUV he'd noticed just moments earlier. "We have a little time, how about we check out this magic show?"

"A magic show? Really? Oh, Mom, can we?" Lucy jumped up and down with excitement. "Please?"

"Sure." Lauren took the brochure he offered and scanned the information. "Looks like fun."

He crossed to the hostess stand and asked how far the theater was from the restaurant. Since it was only four blocks away, he thought it was best to walk.

There was no sign of the SUV when they headed outside a few minutes later. It didn't take them long to get to the theater. He purchased three tickets, then hustled Lucy and Lauren inside.

Much like the brief reprieve they'd gotten while making the snowman, it was clear Lucy appreciated the ability to do something fun. At least for an hour, the worries of the shooter, the frantic escape from the farm, and the threat of kidnapping faded away. In Grady's opinion, the illusionist show was decent, although there were a few times Grady easily figured out the trick. He kept his thoughts to himself, knowing there was no reason to spoil the magic for Lucy.

"That was so fun," Lucy gushed, when it was over. "Can we see the show again tonight?"

"No, Lucy." Lauren spoke in her no-nonsense mom tone. "We're going to head home very soon."

Grady wanted to argue, but at that moment, his phone rang. Seeing Agent Braun's number on the screen, he showed it to Lauren, then answered. "Agent Braun, this is McFarland. What's going on?"

"We have him," Agent Braun got straight to the point. "We have Curtis Handover in custody."

"I'm glad you found him," he said out loud for Lauren's benefit. The relief in her blue eyes was unmistakable. "Is he talking?"

"No, unfortunately, he's lawyered up. If you ask me, that just means he's guilty," Braun said with glee. "He asked for his lawyer the moment the state patrol pulled him over."

Grady wanted to ask more, to understand the timeline, but heard voices in the background.

"I have to go, McFarland, I'll let you know how it goes." With that, Braun ended the call.

"They have him? It's really over?" Lauren asked.

"They have him in custody, but he's not talking." He didn't want to go into more detail with Lucy standing there listening. "Maybe we should stay here tonight, rather than heading back to the city."

"No, Grady, will you please take us home?" Lauren put her hand on his arm. "I need to make sure the penthouse window is fixed and talk to Clara and my father." She flushed, and added, "There's still time for us to make the charity event. If you don't mind sticking around for a while."

Attending the charity ball was the last thing he wanted to do, but he reluctantly nodded. "Of course. I think it's best if we stick together until we know for sure that Curtis Handover has confessed."

"Thank you." Lauren impulsively hugged him, and for a moment, it felt like they were engaged for real. Then she stepped back, smiling brightly. "Let's go then. I'll make some arrangements while we drive."

"Okay." He escorted them outside. Out of habit, he looked for a black SUV but didn't see one. When they reached the car, he drove out of the cute town and headed for the interstate.

But the timeline of Curtis Handover's arrest and the black SUV shooting at them as they escaped via the crop-duster plane niggled at him. Sure, they'd spent a little over two hours in Lake Geneva after leaving the Madison airport, but it still seemed too soon for Curtis to have driven back into Illinois to be arrested by the state patrol.

And why had the guy driven back toward Chicago? Braun hadn't mentioned an accomplice in the arrest, so Grady assumed Handover had been alone. Had the two men argued after losing them at the farmer's field? That was the only thing he could think of that would cause the two men to go their separate ways.

His thoughts continued to whirl in his head. Curtis might have asked for a lawyer so he could make a deal, agreeing to testify against the second shooter for a lesser sentence.

Yet Grady knew he wouldn't be able to relax until they knew for sure who Curtis Handover was working with and that both perps were in custody.

And if that meant attending the charity ball, then fine. He'd put on a monkey suit and attend, for Lauren's and Lucy's sake.

~

LAUREN SPOKE TO CLARA, who thankfully had everything under control as usual. Her super-efficient housekeeper had already arranged for the penthouse window repair and gladly agreed to arrange for a tux to be delivered for Grady. When she asked Grady his size, he didn't look overjoyed but provided the measurements she needed.

"I'm so glad you and Lucy are on your way home," Clara gushed. "Do you want me to stay overnight tonight to watch Lucy?"

She hesitated, debating the pros and cons of doing that. Clara was sweet to stay overnight when Lauren had late-night charity events, but she wasn't sure she wanted to leave her daughter home with Clara. Not when Curtis Handover hadn't confessed to shooting at them or to kidnapping Ariel.

Besides, she could tell from Grady's grim features he wasn't convinced the incidents were over. Agent Braun had mentioned having Curtis in custody, but what about the second man who'd been helping him? Was he still out there somewhere? That thought alone was enough to sway her decision. "No need to stay, Clara. Lucy won't like it, but she can attend the ball with me. I mean, with us."

"Okay, but I'm here if you change your mind," Clara said. "How long before you get here?"

"I'm not sure. You know how traffic gets congested in the city." She felt certain they'd get home just in time to change and leave for the ball. "If you don't mind, set our things out before you leave."

"Oh, I'll stay until you get here. Drive safely."

"We will. Take care, Clara." Lauren lowered the phone.

"I'm surprised she arranged for the window to be repaired," Grady said.

"She has access to our expense account." When Grady arched a brow, she hastily added, "Clara is trustworthy. We have never had a problem with her spending too much money."

"Okay, okay." He shook his head wryly. "My friend Joel Sullivan has a housekeeper on their ranch who they trust with that sort of thing too. I guess I've never had someone I trusted that way."

She eyed him curiously. "You must trust your boss."

"I do, and my former army teammates." Grady paused, then added, "I would trust any of them with my life, as they've always had my back. But living in my house and paying for things isn't the same thing."

"I guess not." Lauren had never been targeted by a gunman like this before. Being kidnapped by Jerry Cromwell when she was a child had been a terrifying experience. One that had made her wary of her daughter suffering the same fate. Yet Jerry hadn't hurt her, he'd just wanted money.

The two gunmen who'd tried to shoot down the crop-duster plane as they'd escaped the farm had gone to extreme efforts to get her daughter. To the point she wasn't even sure this was about money for Curtis and his accomplice anymore.

Curtis must have done this out of revenge. When the kidnapping hadn't worked, and shooting at the penthouse hadn't caused the car crash, he'd given up on the kidnapping idea to simply kill them all instead.

Difficult to understand that logic, but she felt certain Agent Braun would find the evidence he needed to put Curtis and his accomplice in prison for the rest of their lives.

Which made her think about how Nelson was scheduled to get out of jail sooner than she'd anticipated. There's been too many other things to worry about, but now that the danger was over, her ex-husband's release flashed front and center in her mind.

Would Nelson sue for joint custody of Lucy? She wanted to believe he'd move on with his life, but with few job prospects and no money, she felt certain he'd be all over her to get access to his daughter.

"What's wrong?" Grady put his hand on her knee, his expression full of concern. "You look upset."

"I'm fine." She forced a smile. Her concerns about her ex-husband's release and his intent toward their daughter wasn't Grady's problem. Their fake engagement likely wouldn't extend beyond the weekend. "Just glad to be heading home."

He tipped his head to the side as if he wasn't buying her explanation, but he didn't press for more. Instead, he changed the subject. "What time is this charity deal?"

"The cocktail hour is at six; dinner is at seven." She didn't mention the open bar, simply because she didn't drink. And somehow, she didn't think Grady would indulge either. Not when he was there to watch over her and Lucy.

"So if we get there before seven, we'll be fine." He nodded. "Okay, I think we can make that happen. I take it Lucy is coming with us?"

"Yes—"

"I don't wanna go to the charity ball," Lucy interrupted with a wail. "I hate those things. Can't I stay home and watch a movie with Clara?"

"Not tonight." She and Grady spoke at the same time, which made her smile. She turned in her seat to look at Lucy. "Grady was nice enough to take you to see the magic show, right? And maybe you can have a friend over tomorrow. We'll see how things go."

"But I hate those charity things," Lucy repeated, her lower lip stuck out in a pout. "They're boring."

"Hey, I'm going to be there too," Grady said. "And you don't hear me complaining."

Lauren glanced at him, realizing he wasn't necessarily thrilled to be attending the event either. She turned away to stare out the passenger-side window. There was no reason to be upset by his reaction. She and Grady weren't dating. Their relationship wasn't real.

And it never would be.

Their brief kiss seemed like eons ago. No doubt he'd kissed her out of some misguided attempt to make her feel better about the danger they were in.

Whatever. She might have grown to care about Grady, but that was her problem. Not his. She'd always known he would be heading off to another job once she and Lucy didn't need him anymore.

They made good time until they got closer to the city. She knew it didn't really matter if they were late for the ball, but as it turned out, Grady pulled up to the parking garage entrance of her building at 5:45.

That left them plenty of time to get dressed and catch a limo or a taxi to the Cultural Center for the ball.

"Good evening, Ms. Lauren." The security guard peered into Grady's open driver's side window. "Everything okay?"

"Yes, Timothy, we're fine, thanks for asking." She knew the security guard was just being overly cautious. "This is my fiancé, Grady McFarland."

"Nice to meet you, Grady," Timothy said politely.

"Nice to meet you too," Grady said with a grin. "I appreciate you looking out for Lauren and Lucy. They're very important to me."

"Of course. You have a wonderful evening." Timothy Freeman leaned back and opened the gate. Grady drove into the parking garage to her usual parking spot.

"Thanks for treating Timothy with respect." She realized that Nelson's snide approach to the working class should have been another giant red flag.

Grady arched a brow. "Always."

She pushed out of the car, then opened the back door for Lucy. Her daughter was still pouting about being forced to attend the ball, but Lauren ignored her. Someday, Lucy would understand that there were worse things in the world than being forced to attend a boring charity event.

They took the elevator to the penthouse apartment. As Lauren used the key to unlock the door, Clara was there to greet them. "Welcome home."

"Thanks, Clara." She gave the housekeeper a quick hug. "And thanks for getting everything ready for us."

"I take it that's my tux?" Grady asked, eyeing the suit that was draped over the sofa.

"Yes, Mr. Grady. If you need anything altered, let me know." Clara beamed. "I'm handy with a needle and thread."

"I'm sure it will be fine." Grady crossed over to pick up the suit. "I'll change in the guest room."

"Ms. Lauren, I have your dress and Lucy's laid out in your room," Clara said. "I assumed you wanted the red dress."

"Yes, thanks, Clara." She turned to Lucy. "Let's go, Lucy."

Her daughter rolled her eyes and sighed dramatically. "There's still time for you to change your mind, Mom."

"Let's go," she repeated sternly. "I mean it, Lucy. I'm tired too. I promise we won't stay for the entire ball, just long enough to mingle a bit before dinner. We'll come home right afterward, okay?"

"Fine." Lucy dragged her feet as they headed into Lauren's room. Then her daughter brightened. "Oh, I get to wear a red dress too?"

"Yes, you're going to look beautiful." She was glad Clara had remembered this charity was for the pediatric cardiac care program at St. Mary's Children's Hospital. Hence the red dresses. "Give me a minute to change and I'll help you."

Fifteen minutes later, she and Lucy were ready to go. Normally, Lauren would have had her hair done special, and Lucy's too, but that couldn't be helped. It was nothing short of a miracle that they were back in time to attend at all.

When she and Lucy stepped into the living room, she stopped short upon seeing Grady standing there in his tuxedo. If she thought he was attractive before, with his longish dark-brown hair and five o'clock shadow, he was downright gorgeous now.

"Wow." He whistled. "Lauren, you and Lucy look amazing."

"Thank you." She felt herself blush, even though she knew he was just playing along with his role. "And you look dashing yourself. I really appreciate you escorting us tonight."

"Absolutely." His eyes narrowed a bit. "There's been no word from Agent Braun. I left him another message. Hopefully, he'll call back soon."

"He will." She forced herself to sound confident. She imagined Braun was working out a deal with Curtis Handover at this very moment.

"I know." Grady stepped forward and picked up her long leather coat, holding it so she could slip her arms into the sleeves.

"Thanks." She hoped couldn't help but smile when Grady held Lucy's coat for her too. Ever the gentleman. More so than Nelson ever was.

When Grady offered his arm, she tucked her hand in the curve of his elbow. Glancing up at his handsome profile, she wished again that this were a real date.

Apparently, she was destined to be like a reversal of Cinderella. She wasn't poor, and she would have her night at the ball. But at the stroke of midnight, Grady would cease to be her Prince Charming. Tomorrow, he would be gone.

Leaving her and Lucy alone once again.

13

———

ow Grady managed to utter a coherent sentence
was beyond him. He'd nearly swallowed his
tongue when Lauren glided into the living room
wearing a form-fitting sequined red dress, Lucy at her side.
And glided was the right word. Lauren looked as if she were
walking on air.

She was the most beautiful woman he'd ever known,
and for what felt like the zillionth time, he had to force
himself to remember his job was to protect her and Lucy.

Not to kiss her again.

It was no wonder she pulled in so much money for her
charity events. He would donate everything he had just to
spend time with her.

As Grady escorted Lauren and Lucy out of the penthouse and to the elevator, he tried not to remember that
she'd asked him to act as her fiancé for the evening. Better
that he focus on his role as their bodyguard.

"I have a car waiting outside the lobby," Lauren said as
she pushed the elevator button.

He arched a brow. "When did you arrange that?"

"Months ago." She looked confused by his question. "I use the same car service for all my charity events."

Her world was beyond his comprehension. He couldn't imagine having a car service set up that far in advance. And the more he thought about her following her usual routine, the more he didn't like it.

"Hold on. I think it's better if I drive the rental." He frowned when Lauren looked annoyed. "I'm sure the hotel has valet parking, right?"

"Yes. But I always take the limo . . ." Her voice trailed off as she suddenly realized his concern. "Okay, fine. You can drive, but I need to tell the driver so he's not sitting there for hours."

"We can do that." As the elevator slid down to the lobby level, and the doors slowly opened, he swept a curious gaze around the area. He'd only been in the parking garage and up in the penthouse. The décor was fancier than he'd anticipated. Lots of chrome and glass, with floor-to-ceiling windows overlooking the street. There was a front desk manned by a security guard who nodded at them as they walked past. There were also several cushioned chairs scattered about. Savion Enterprises was an impressive place.

And Grady knew it was only one of many properties her father owned.

A long black limo sat outside the front doors. Grady glanced at Lauren. "Stay here with Lucy, I'll tell him to go."

"Earl isn't going to listen to you." Lauren rolled her eyes. "Lucy, wait here by the main desk. I'll be right back." She strode to the main doors. Grady made sure to stay close at her side. A cold wind blew in as she stepped out to the limo. Grady scanned the street on the off chance the black SUV was still out there somewhere, but it was too dark to make out the make and model of the vehicles driving past. Traffic was still congested, and he was struck again by how different Chicago was from Cody, Wyoming.

"Ms. Lauren." Earl looked to be in his early seventies, but the way the older man eyed him suspiciously was oddly reassuring. Grady was glad she had someone like Earl looking out for her.

"Hi, Earl, I'm so sorry, but I won't need your services today."

The older man scowled. "Are you sure about this?" There was no doubt Earl didn't like the change of plan.

"I'm Grady McFarland." Grady stepped forward and offered his hand. "I'm sorry for the switch, but I'll be driving Lauren and Lucy to the charity tonight."

Earl gripped his hand strongly, nodding slowly. Maybe because of the handshake, but the older man's suspicions had eased off a bit. "Nice to meet you. Okay, then. I'll be here tomorrow, Ms. Lauren, unless you change your mind."

"Thanks, Earl. You're the best." Lauren flashed Earl a warm smile, then turned to go back inside. Lucy stood waiting by the front desk as requested.

Grady escorted them to the elevator, where they went down to the underground parking garage. As he had earlier, he scanned the parked cars around the rental. He recognized a couple of cars as being there the day before, likely people living in various apartments within the building. No black SUVs with tinted windows, though.

Maybe Agent Braun had the right perp in custody. It could be that Curtis Handover had been the mastermind behind the kidnapping and shooting events, driven by revenge along with more cash than the guy could make in his lifetime. And with Handover out of the picture, his accomplice may have skipped down.

Or be hiding somewhere, waiting for Handover to be released on bail. Depending on the evidence the feds had on the guy, it was possible Handover would be released until the feds built their case against him.

A possibility he wasn't about to confide to Lauren. She'd been through enough trauma at this point. He'd wait until they heard from Agent Braun with an update.

Hopefully no later than tomorrow morning.

He opened the car doors for Lauren and Lucy, then slid in behind the wheel. He kept a keen eye out for anyone suspicious, just in case Handover's accomplice was waiting nearby with the intent to finish the job.

"Do you know where the Chicago Cultural Center is located?" Lauren asked as he exited the parking garage.

"Not exactly." He belatedly realized they should have replaced their phones while they were in Lake Geneva. "Can you give me directions?"

"Yes. Turn left at the next intersection."

They inched with maddening slowness through the congested city streets. There were several black SUVs, and he found himself tensing up every time one of them got too close. But the drivers behind the wheels didn't look at them twice.

After the third false alarm, he tried to relax, flexing his fingers from the deathlike grip on the wheel. He doubted a high-profile charity event would be considered a good time to try kidnapping a child.

By the time they arrived at the Cultural Center, Grady understood why Lauren had a car service pretty much on standby. He figured he could have walked the distance in the same amount of time it took to drive there.

As they waited in line for the valet attendant, he glanced at Lauren. "Anything I need to know about the people who will be here tonight?"

She glanced back at Lucy, then shrugged. "There are a few persistent men who I'd love for you to keep away from me. But otherwise, it's just a fancy dinner."

"I hate fancy dinners," Lucy muttered.

Lauren sighed. "I know you do, and I appreciate you being on your best behavior, young lady."

"Yeah, yeah," Lucy reluctantly agreed. "Smile and be polite."

"Exactly." Lauren nodded at the red taillights moving up ahead. "You're next."

"I know." He eased forward. When the next valet attendant bent to look inside, the kid's eyes widened when he saw Lauren.

"Ms. Chandler." The kid ran around to open her door. "I didn't realize you were arriving on your own tonight."

"Hello, Tony. Yes, my fiancé, Grady McFarland, wanted to do the honors." She smiled brightly at the kid. "And we've brought my daughter, Lucy, with us too."

The young kid hastily opened the back door for Lucy. Grady had to admit it was nice that Lauren was so well known by the people who worked at these venues. No doubt she'd been there dozens of times before.

He handed the kid the keys and hurried around to escort Lauren and Lucy inside. As they stopped to remove their winter coats, he tried to pretend he'd done this before, but the glitz and glamour were as foreign to him as the sandy and deadly desert of Afghanistan would have been to Lauren.

The environment was slightly better, but Grady didn't doubt that there were many wolves dressed in fine clothing pretending to be upstanding citizens in the crowd.

The party was in full swing by the time they entered the grand ballroom. It was a little like being with royalty as the moment Lauren stepped into the room several people rushed forward, gushing with enthusiasm.

"Oh, Lauren, you look stunning as always. And you brought Lucy too!" The woman who'd gotten there first eyed him with a mixture of admiration and suspicion. "And you have a guest!"

"Good to see you again, Patrice. This is my fiancé, Grady McFarland. Grady, Patrice Miller is the vice president of St. Mary's Children's Hospital."

"You're engaged!" Despite her role as a hospital vice president, Patrice squealed with joy. "That's marvelous news! Where did you meet?"

"We share friends in common, Suzanne and Eli White," Grady said, remembering Lauren mentioning them.

"Well congratulations! I know a few of the male atten- dees will be devastated to hear you're taken." Patrice eyed him with glee. "I'm so pleased to meet you, Mr. McFarland."

"Likewise." Grady forced a smile and tried not to tug at his tie that suddenly felt too tight. If he were a drinking man, he'd belly up to the bar. But he wasn't, so he did his best to stay alert as they made their way through the crowd.

A waiter walked by with a tray of champagne flutes. He shook his head, noticing Lauren did the same.

"What do you usually drink at these shindigs?" he asked in a low voice.

"Ginger ale." She smiled up at him. "You hate this, don't you?"

"Nah, I've been in worse places." He hadn't realized his feelings were telegraphed on his face. "I'll get us some ginger ale. Excuse me." He patted her hand, then slipped through the throng of people, many who stared at him with blatant curiosity.

No doubt news of his and Lauren's engagement had already zipped like a live wire through the crowd, and these rich people were wondering how he'd snagged the prettiest girl in the room.

If this were a real engagement, they'd have every right to wonder. He tugged at his tie, then smiled at the bartender as he requested three glasses of ginger ale, assuming Lucy would want one as well.

Carrying the three glasses together pressed together, he made his way over to a table where Lucy and Lauren were waiting. Lucy was seated at the table and glanced up at him as he set the soft drink in front of her. "Thank you."

"You're welcome." He handed a second glass to Lauren. "I take it we're sitting here?"

"Yes, this is the head table. Patrice and her husband, Aaron, will be here too." She sipped her soft drink, then set it beside her daughter. "Lucy, why don't you wait here? I need to say hi to a few more people before we sit down to eat."

"Bor-ring." Lucy sighed theatrically, then lifted her glass to drink down all her ginger ale in one long gulp. "Fine. I'll wait here."

"Thank you." Lauren slipped her arm around his waist. "And thank you, too, for going along with the charade."

"Hey, I'm getting a kick out of the way some of these guys are staring at me with faces that literally glow green with envy." He winked and wrapped his arm around her shoulders. "Lead on, my love."

Lauren stumbled a bit but then regained her footing. He was about to ask if she was okay, when she said, "As soon as we finish eating dinner, we can head home. There's no reason to stay for the dancing."

Personally, he'd have loved to stay for the dancing, but he understood she wanted to make her presence known before getting Lucy home at a reasonable hour. "Whatever you want to do is fine with me. What sort of meal can we expect anyway? Rubbery chicken?"

She laughed. "How did you know? Have you been to charity dinners before? They're always serving some variation of a baked chicken dish. Just once I wish they'd throw in a salmon or some other entrée."

He didn't answer, his gaze narrowing on a man with sleekly combed blond hair striding purposefully toward them. The guy's gaze seemed to be boring into Lauren's.

"Oh no," Lauren whispered, her arm around his waist tightening. "I guess Ethan has heard the news."

Grady understood this guy must have been one of her dogged admirers. He stopped, pulled her around so she was fully in his arms, then leaned in to capture her mouth with his.

Lauren surprised him by leaning into his embrace, returning his kiss with enough heat to send the entire ballroom up in flames. He'd intended this to be a simple warning to Ethan, whoever he was, but instantly, everything around them faded into oblivion.

In that moment, Grady knew he was dangerously close to falling in love with Lauren Chandler. A disaster of epic proportions, as they were complete opposites in every way. He couldn't imagine living in a penthouse apartment in the middle of the city, and Lauren wouldn't be comfortable in anything less.

And there was Lucy to consider too.

This intense attraction between them couldn't lead to

anything long term. Forcing himself to face reality, Grady reluctantly lifted his head, ending their kiss.

For a long moment, Lauren gazed up at him with a dreamy expression. Then she seemed to realize where they were and glanced around guiltily.

The guy, Ethan whomever, had veered away, heading straight for the bar. From the way the guy tossed back his drink, he'd accepted their engagement at face value and was about to drown his sorrows in booze.

Leaving Grady to wonder just what Ethan might do when he'd left Lauren and Lucy behind to head back to Cody, Wyoming.

INWARDLY REELING from the dizzying impact of Grady's kiss, it took all of Lauren's willpower not to throw herself into Grady's arms again.

His kiss was more potent than anything she'd experienced before. Obviously, Grady's impulsive embrace had been intended to put on a show for Ethan Whitman. To seal the news of their engagement in an announcement for the entire room.

Not because he'd wanted to kiss her.

Her heart thumped erratically against her sternum as she struggled to maintain control. Thankfully, Ethan had gotten the message loud and clear. He was at the bar, drinking heavily the way Nelson used to do.

Obviously, she never should have married Nelson. Her ex-husband's kisses hadn't been nearly as amazing as Grady's. If she'd met Grady first, she'd never have settled for Nelson. But with all the praying she'd done over the past day and a half, she had to admit that God had sent Nelson to her for a reason. One, to realize what she didn't want in a man. More importantly, though, her union with Nelson had produced Lucy.

And her daughter was the most important person in the world.

Too bad, she wouldn't have more children. Unless, of course, she was blessed enough to meet another man like Grady, who could make her blush with a simple smile and a wink.

Yeah, that probably wasn't going to happen.

A waiter came by with a tray of shrimp. To give herself a moment, Lauren accepted the appetizer and popped the shrimp into her mouth.

"I don't think he'll be bothering you again," Grady drawled near her ear.

She almost choked on the shrimp. Hastily swallowing, she managed a smile. "Thanks. Ethan has been incredibly persistent. No matter how many times I've told him I'm not ready to date again."

Grady frowned, glancing again at Ethan who had another drink in his hand. The way Ethan kept his back to them made her think of a little boy fuming in the corner of the classroom. "Do you think he could do something as crazy as hiring someone to kidnap your daughter?"

She stared up at him in exasperation. "Agent Braun has arrested Curtis Handover for the kidnapping and shooting incidents. Besides, that's not Ethan's style. He thinks I should be interested in him because he's handsome and comes from wealth too." She'd been shocked when Ethan had bad-mouthed Nelson for marrying her for her money. She hadn't realized that the entire social circle had known what she'd failed to discern on her own.

"Doesn't mean he wouldn't stoop to playing dirty," Grady muttered. "He looks like a sore loser if you ask me."

That made her smile. "You'd be right about that."

"Is there anyone else I need to know about?" Grady looked as if he wouldn't mind pulling his weapon to show her overzealous admirers who's in charge.

"Ethan Whitman is the worst of the bunch. Alex Tillman is a close second." She scanned the patrons clustered around the bar. "I see Alex. He's chatting with the mayor." With a sigh, she forced a smile. One of the reasons she'd wanted Grady to pretend to be her fiancé was because she wanted these guys to leave her alone. The best way to do that was to show Grady off. "Come on, I'll introduce you."

"Can't wait," Grady drawled. When he slipped his arm around her waist, she felt the heat of his touch through her sequined dress.

"Mayor Thompson, it's good to see you again." Lauren addressed the mayor first, then turned to Alex. "Alex, I'd like you and the mayor to meet my fiancé, Grady McFarland. Grady, this is Alex Tillman and Mayor Bart Thompson."

"A pleasure to meet you both." Grady released her to offer his hand to the mayor first, then Alex. Alex masked his annoyance, but she could tell he wasn't happy about the news of their engagement.

"McFarland?" Alex echoed with a snooty look at Grady. "I don't remember hearing your name before. You must be new around here."

"I am," Grady admitted cheerfully. Then he put his arm around her shoulders, and added, "Lauren is amazing, isn't she?"

"Yeah." Alex tossed back the rest of his drink. "Excuse me."

Lauren watched him go with a sense of relief. It was

depressing to know that in a few weeks or so, she'd have to acknowledge that she and Grady had broken things off to go their separate ways. Having Grady at her side, keeping the leeches like Ethan and Alex away, was a temporary arrangement.

And really, it was a sad state of affairs that she had been put in this position of asking Grady to do this favor in the first place. A flash of anger hit hard. Why should she have to put up with their boorish behavior anyway? There was no reason for either of these men to keep hounding her. As if their persistence alone would change her mind.

She turned and scanned the room, looking for Lucy. Earlier, when they'd been at the table, she'd noticed a waiter hovering nearby who'd looked familiar. There was something about his eyes that had niggled at her memory. Obviously, she must have seen him at one of these charity events before but hated to admit she normally didn't pay close attention to the serving staff. Not that she considered them beneath her, because she didn't. Her goal of sponsoring this event was so that anyone, from a homeless person to a CEO, would have the best cardiac care for their children. The simple truth was that the waitstaff didn't wear name tags, and there were literally dozens of them at each event.

Lucy was still at the table, swinging her legs back and forth, and she looked bored to tears. She was about to suggest they head over to keep her daughter company when Grady's phone rang.

With a frown, he pulled it from his pocket. He eyed the screen, then said, "It's Agent Braun."

"Maybe Curtis confessed?" As much as she enjoyed Grady's company, she was anxious for the danger to be over. "Answer it."

"This is McFarland," he said into the phone. If they

weren't standing in the middle of the ballroom, she'd have asked him to put the call on speaker.

She held her breath as Grady's expression turned to stone. Then he turned toward her, shaking his head. Her heart sank. Apparently, Curtis Handover hadn't confessed.

But that didn't mean he wasn't still guilty.

"Thanks for letting us know." Grady waited another beat, then added, "I agree that reviewing the video is the best way to find them. Lauren and I would appreciate another update in the morning."

A moment later, he'd pocketed the cheap phone. Obviously, the news from the FBI wasn't good. "Just tell me, Grady. What happened?"

"A number of things." He sighed. "Curtis Handover has an alibi for the time frame of the Ariel's abduction. They also searched his home and his car for a weapon and other evidence but didn't find anything to tie him to the recent shooting attempts against us. He finally agreed to talk to them. While he insists he holds Nelson responsible for his half brother's death, he isn't angry at you." Grady raked a hand through his wavy dark hair in a frustrated gesture. "He's not our guy."

"Maybe his accomplice is the one with the weapon?" She hated knowing the kidnapper might still be out there, intending to harm her daughter. "We saw both men standing outside the SUV when we escaped in the crop-duster plane."

Grady shrugged. "Anything is possible, but it sounds like Agent Braun has decided to believe Curtis when he says he's not involved. They let him go, as they had nothing to hold him on. And as you heard, they're planning to resume the task of reviewing toll camera footage to find the black SUV with tinted windows with the partial plate we've provided."

"That could take forever."

"I know. But don't worry. They'll find him." Grady's words lacked the confidence she was accustomed to hearing from him. "I'll call Griff later, once we get home."

"Okay." She tried to push the cloud of depression away. "I guess it's a good thing we kept Lucy with us tonight."

"Yeah." He nodded toward the bar. "Would you like more ginger ale?"

"No thanks." She answered absently, then added, "Although Lucy would probably like one."

"I'm happy to head up to the bar," Grady offered. He winked, his expression lightening despite the distressing turn of events. "It might be fun to introduce myself to your buddy Ethan."

"Please don't bother. Knowing Ethan, he'll be incredibly rude to you." She turned to scan the room. "Wait a minute, where is Lucy? I don't see her sitting at the head table anymore. She was there a few minutes ago."

"Maybe she went to get another ginger ale?" Grady suggested. "Or she could have gone to the ladies' room."

"I told her to stay at the table." She pushed past Grady to head in that direction. She understood Lucy was bored with the formal dinner environment, but that didn't mean her daughter should be wandering around the ballroom bothering the guests.

A man in a waiter uniform was striding toward a door near the far side of the room. Lauren frowned as she caught a hint of a red dress.

Lucy's dress?

She reached out to grab Grady's arm. "I think that waiter kidnapped Lucy!"

His expression turned grim as he reached for his weapon. "Stay here. I'll go after them."

No way was she staying put. As Grady broke into a run, dodging guests as he headed toward the side door where Lauren had assumed the kitchen staging area was located, she lifted her skirt and hurried to keep up.

Praying with all her heart that the kidnapper wouldn't hurt Lucy before Grady could get there.

14

Weapon in hand, Grady bolted toward the door where the waiter had disappeared with Lucy, mentally kicking himself for lowering his guard. Just because the ballroom was full of rich people didn't mean it was a safe environment. He should have anticipated Curtis Handover wasn't their kidnapper.

If anything bad happened to Lucy, he'd never forgive himself.

Bursting through the door, Grady found himself in a narrow hallway. The sound of dishes clanking together indicated the kitchen was nearby. Catching a glimpse of the waiter carrying Lucy toward another door, he put on a burst of speed to catch up.

"Stop!" he shouted, wishing he could claim to be a police officer.

The waiter ignored him.

"Grady! Mommy! Help me!" Lucy's cry stabbed his heart.

Closing the distance, he swallowed hard, knowing he didn't dare fire a round. Not when the guy held Lucy so close.

"We're coming, Lucy," Lauren shouted from behind him. He didn't look back, his gaze fixated on the waiter who had already reached the door on the other end of the hallway. Grady had no idea what was on the other side, but he knew the kidnapper likely had an accomplice.

Two people had orchestrated these attempts.

"Mommy!" Lucy screamed when the waiter pushed through the door. Then Lucy reached out to grab the doorframe, trying to hold on.

Grady did his best to close the gap between them, despite their head start. Unfortunately, the little girl wasn't strong enough to hold on for long. She sobbed as her fingers slipped free.

Then they were gone. Through the door to whatever waited on the other side.

"Lucy!" Lauren's scream bounced off the walls of the narrow hallway. Grady leaped forward and pushed through the door. To his surprise, he was on a small landing of a stairwell. He should have gotten a blueprint of the building prior to this event, but he hadn't.

A lapse in judgment that might cost Lucy her life.

The thudding of footsteps and the heartbreaking sound of Lucy's sobs echoed through the stairwell. The exit sign on the wall indicated this set of stairs was a fire exit, meaning it would eventually lead to the outside.

Grady flew down the stairs after them, praying he'd reach them before they made it all the way out of the building. He wished he could tell Lauren there was likely a car waiting outside for the kidnapper and Lucy, but there wasn't a second to waste. He couldn't lose them!

When he heard a door opening, his heart sank. He turned on a half landing, then took the last flight of stairs down to the ground level. He jumped, skipping the last six stairs just as the outside door closed behind the waiter and Lucy.

Slamming into the door, he burst through. His gut instinct was right. The black SUV was sitting in the alley. The back passenger door was open, and the waiter was shoving Lucy inside.

"Stop!" Now that the guy wasn't holding Lucy near his body, Grady lifted his weapon and fired two shots.

Both hit their mark.

The waiter screamed and crumpled to the ground. But the driver of the black car hit the gas and took off down the alley. The swift movement of the car caused the door to swing closed, trapping Lucy inside.

No! They were getting away!

Grady leaped over the fallen man and ran after the car. He couldn't see Lucy and prayed she wasn't hurt. He memorized the license plate and hoped the traffic was congested enough on the road that he could catch up.

The brake lights flashed as the car slowed. He sprinted forward, slamming his hands on the back window. Lucy's face popped into view. Tears streamed down her face, and he could hear her muffled cry.

"Grady!"

The driver cranked the wheel. Horns blared as the SUV carelessly merged into traffic. Grady stayed with the vehicle for another few feet, until a driver in one of the cars the kidnapper had cut off rammed into him, sending him stumbling.

No, no, no! His hip burned with pain from the driver of the car striking him. He had to move out of the way to avoid being hit again. The driver of the black SUV used the opportunity to escape. The kidnapper wedged his car between two other cars, causing more blaring car horns.

They were in the center lane now, which made it impossible for him to follow on foot.

Making his way to the side of the road, he pulled out his phone and called 911. The dispatcher seemed to take forever to answer, but when she did, he kept his voice as calm as possible.

"There's a black Honda Pilot SUV heading south on Michigan Avenue heading away from the Chicago Cultural Center. License plate is RTK3002. The driver has abducted a seven-year-old girl named Lucy Chandler. I need Chicago PD to send multiple units to this location right away."

"I'll send the police officers to your location. What is your name?"

"Grady McFarland." He stared out at the myriads of tail-lights, fearing the police response would be too little, too late.

A wave of horror washed over him. He'd failed in his mission to keep Lucy safe from harm in the worst way possible.

And Lauren would have every right to hate him for it.

Lauren had kicked off her ridiculous heels to follow Grady down the stairs. Yet it wasn't easy to maneuver with the long dress she wore. Reaching the ground level, she pushed outside. Then stopped abruptly, covering her mouth in horror when she saw the waiter lying on the ground in a pool of blood.

She rushed forward, the cold ground freezing the bottoms of her feet, to kneel beside the fallen man. She put a hand to his neck to feel for a pulse.

There wasn't one. His skin was pale and already feeling cool to the touch.

Staring at the dead kidnapper's face, she tried to understand why he'd looked so familiar. Had she seen him before? Maybe in passing? There was something about his eyes, but she still couldn't place him. Pushing herself upright, she glanced down the alley, searching for Grady and Lucy.

Her heart sank to the soles of her frozen feet when she saw Grady limping toward her. His expression was a mask of anger and frustration. She searched his gaze. "What happened? Where's Lucy?"

"I called the police and reported the license plate number to the black Honda SUV." He sighed. "I'm sorry. I tried to keep up with the car, but some guy ran into me. The black SUV merged into the center lane to escape."

Escape? The kidnapper had Lucy? Tears filled her eyes. *No, please Lord Jesus. No!* This couldn't be happening.

But it was. Lauren wanted to scream and cry out in rage, but that wouldn't help find her daughter. She whirled away, turning her back on Grady to call Agent Braun, who thankfully answered on the first ring. "The kidnappers have Lucy."

"Where are you?" To his credit, Agent Braun sounded concerned.

"Outside the Chicago Cultural Center." She swiped at her eyes. Two police cars with their red and blue lights flashing were heading toward them, moving slowly as they wedged through traffic. "Grady shot one of the kidnappers, but he's dead."

"I'll be there as soon as possible." The line went dead, and she turned when Grady came up to stand beside her.

She pushed the words through her tight throat. "Agent Braun is on his way."

Grady nodded grimly. "I've called Rex too. He's sending another guardian to take over."

She frowned. "What do you mean? I don't want anyone else. I need you to help us find Lucy!"

He jutted his chin toward the cops who'd pulled up in front of the alley, blocking it off. She belatedly realized the alley was a crime scene. "I shot and killed a man. I'm going to be tied up for a while."

"No." She reached out to grasp his arm. "You shot that man because he was kidnapping Lucy. I need you. We must find the driver of that car."

Confusion flickered in his gaze. "It's my fault she's gone."

Fresh tears filled her eyes. "No, it's my fault. I'm the one who insisted on attending this ball. I thought . . ." She couldn't finish. She'd believed Agent Braun had the kidnapper in custody.

And now her daughter would pay the price of her gross error in judgment.

"I failed to keep Lucy safe," Grady insisted. "I carry the blame here, not you."

She shook her head and swiped at her eyes. It was nice of him to take the heat, but she knew she should have stayed home with Lucy and Grady.

She shivered and belatedly realized she couldn't feel her feet. Grady noticed and shrugged out of his tux jacket, draping it around her shoulders. She needed to go inside to find her shoes, but she couldn't bring herself to move. Her discomfort was nothing compared to what Lucy was going through.

A nightmare Lauren knew all too well.

"What happened?" The police officer who approached rested his hand on his weapon.

Grady stepped forward. He offered his weapon to the

cop butt first. "Ms. Lauren Chandler's daughter was kidnapped. I shot that man as he shoved Lucy into the car. The driver of the car took off with Lucy inside. I ran after it, keeping pace until I was struck by another car. The driver of the black SUV managed to get into the left lane, making it impossible for me to continue running alongside without getting crushed in traffic."

The officer's eyes widened in shock, telling Lauren he must have recognized her name. It was one of the rare times it was beneficial to be wealthy. He took the weapon Grady offered, and it was all she could do not to cry out in protest. She needed Grady to be armed for whatever they faced when it came to getting Lucy back. Then the cop turned to her. "Do you recognize the man who took your daughter?"

"No, but there is something familiar about his eyes." She knew that sounded crazy. "I don't know how to explain it."

"Let's see if he has an ID on him." The officer turned to cross over to the body. A second officer was kneeling beside the fallen man already, doing as she had, making sure he was dead. Wearing gloves, the officer near the body patted the dead man's pockets, then removed a wallet and opened it.

"Who is it?" Grady asked.

"Guy by the name of Shane Cromwell." The officer stared up at her. "Does that sound familiar?"

A wave of dizziness hit hard. She put a hand on Grady's arm to keep herself from collapsing to the ground. No wonder the young waiter's eyes looked familiar. "Yes. Jerry Cromwell was the man who kidnapped me twenty-five years ago. I think Shane must be his son. Or maybe a nephew."

"Does Jerry have other children?" Grady asked, a sense of urgency in his voice.

"I have no idea." She felt as if she'd been sideswiped by a

semitruck. "I didn't know Jerry had kids at all. Last I heard, his wife divorced him after he went to prison. He didn't have kids back then."

"This guy's ID says he's twenty-four years old." The cop rose to his feet. "Could be that Jerry's wife was pregnant when he went to jail. Had the kid after the divorce."

"Run the license plate," Grady said, and repeated the series of letters and numbers. "See if it's owned by Cromwell."

The officer spoke into his radio collar. Through the static, she could hear the dispatcher's response. "The car is registered to Simon Cromwell. According to the registration, he's twenty-four years old. Do you want his address?"

"Yes, give it to me." The officer listened as he looked at what was written on Shane's driver's license. Then he nodded. "Okay, it's a match. They must be brothers."

Again, her knees threatened to buckle. Her baby had been taken by the twin sons of the man who'd kidnapped her twenty-five years ago.

Was this about money? Or revenge?

Likely both. And that scared her the most of all. Jerry Cromwell hadn't physically hurt Lauren back when she'd been taken. All he'd wanted was money. She remembered staring up at his eyes, though. Eyes that he'd passed down to his son.

She had no idea if Simon Cromwell would treat Lucy the same way. Or if he'd hurt the little girl.

All she could do was pray they'd find Lucy very soon.

"Lauren?" Grady's low voice had her turning to face him. He wrapped his arm around her shoulders, giving her a brief hug. "You're shivering. Let's go inside."

"W-what a-bout the p-police?" Her teeth were chattering so much she could barely speak. She couldn't imagine how she'd function if Grady was arrested for killing Shane Cromwell.

"Detective Kramer is here." He nodded to where the detective was talking to the patrol officers. "He said I'm free to go."

That was a relief. She nodded and allowed Grady to walk her back to the doorway. Only to discover it was locked. Her feet were numb, and she stumbled a bit as he steered her toward the front of the building.

"Wait a minute, are you barefoot?" Grady didn't wait for her to answer but swept her into his arms, carrying her like a child. She wanted to protest, but a glimpse at her bloody feet kept her silent.

The doorman let them in. Grady thanked him, then crossed the lobby of the Cultural Center to set her down on a plush chair. She frowned at her blood-stained feet, realizing she must have cut them during her dash down the stairs and outside.

"Stay here. I'll get towels from the bathroom." Grady turned and quickly strode toward the restrooms. She didn't care about her injuries; all she wanted was for Lucy to be returned unharmed.

The police needed to be out there searching for Simon Cromwell and Lucy. Would he be stupid enough to go home? Probably not, but she hoped the police would check there anyway.

It was at that moment that Lauren realized she didn't have her phone. Her real phone, not the disposable one Grady had purchased for them. What if Cromwell called with a ransom demand? She pushed to her feet just as Grady came back holding damp towels in his hands.

The Cultural Center did not use paper towels in their bathrooms.

"Sit down. Let me take care of your feet." Grady narrowed his gaze when she shook her head. "Lauren, please."

"I need to get home to grab my phone for when Simon Cromwell calls with a ransom demand."

"I've thought of that. I asked Rex to bring a replacement device for you in case yours is out of power." He gently pushed her down. "Let me take care of your feet. Then we'll get out of here."

The fact that Grady had already thought of a replacement phone had her sinking back down on the chair. He knelt at her feet, setting her feet on the damp towel. The warm water felt good, but as her toes warmed, she was aware of the stinging sensation from the cuts she'd sustained.

A man wearing a black jacket with bright yellow FBI letters embossed on it strode into the lobby. Glancing over, he quickly headed toward them. Flashing a badge, he said, "I'm Agent Braun. I know you've already gone through this with the local police, but I need to know what happened."

He was roughly her age, maybe a few years older. He wasn't wearing a suit, likely because it was after hours.

Grady filled him in on the events that started in the ballroom and ended outside in the alley outside the building. Lauren was grateful for the warmth, but she was impatient for the police and the FBI to stop talking and to start searching for Lucy.

"Has anyone gone to Simon Cromwell's apartment?" she interrupted, before Grady could finish.

"Officers have been dispatched to that location, yes." Agent Braun sighed. "We also have issued a BOLO for the vehicle."

"I need to make a call." Grady stepped away to use his

disposable phone. Lauren hoped he was calling his FBI friend. She didn't care if Griff was in Wyoming, they needed all the help they could get.

"I'll accompany you back to your home," Braun said. "I have a tech team who will join us so we can put a tap on your cell phone. That's our best chance of locating where this guy is hiding with Lucy."

"Fine." She stood, ignoring the burning sensation in her feet. "Grady? Let's get out of here."

"Thanks, Griff." Grady pocketed his phone and turned to join them. "Griff has his tech guy Dominic searching cameras for the SUV."

Braun frowned. "We have techs working on that too."

"More eyes can't hurt." Grady came over to take her arm. "Are you ready to go? Rex and Mick, I mean, Micah are going to meet us at your penthouse."

"Yes." She didn't hesitate. This nightmare was her fault, but she tried to believe that Cromwell wouldn't hurt Lucy. Not if he just wanted money.

Please, Lord. She swallowed hard, hoping her prayer was being heard as Grady arranged for the valet to have their rental brought around.

The next fifteen minutes passed in a daze. Lauren searched the cars around them for Lucy, even though she knew Simon Cromwell must have had her daughter stashed away somewhere by now. But she couldn't seem to help herself. The congested traffic made her want to scream in frustration When they finally reached the Savion building, her nerves were shot. Grady parked in the same spot as earlier, and they were silent as they rode the elevator to the penthouse.

She walked into the apartment, keenly aware of the emptiness inside. No Clara, and worst of all, no Lucy.

Lauren forced herself to head into the bedroom to change out of her gown. Not that she cared how she looked, but she needed something soft to cover her feet.

She grabbed her phone, only to see that it was dead. She plugged it in, then headed back to the living room. By the time she emerged, she saw that Grady had taken the time to change too. Remembering how handsome he'd looked in his tux made her look away. Her stupidity of insisting on attending the ball had gotten her daughter kidnapped. She couldn't bear to think about how Grady had held her.

Kissed her.

Somehow, Rex and a tall man with blond hair, who she assumed was Micah, arrived a few minutes later. Grady let them in and made introductions she barely acknowledged. She couldn't stop from rushing forward to snatch the new phone Rex held in his hands.

"Thank you." She took the phone and quickly accessed her iCloud account so she could transfer the information over from her old phone number. The one Lucy knew by heart.

It took a few minutes for the missed calls, messages, and text messages to light up the screen. She searched them all quickly, but none were from Simon Cromwell.

Or Lucy.

She sank onto the sofa, staring at her phone. How long would it take for Simon to call? A few minutes? An hour?

Or longer?

Thinking back to when Jerry Cromwell had kidnapped her as a child, she vaguely remembered him giving her father time to get the money together. It hadn't made much sense at the time, but now she understood the impact. Banks were closed now, and it was a Friday night. Some banks had Saturday morning hours, but to get the kind of cash Simon would ask for would be impossible.

Something he and his twin brother obviously hadn't considered before grabbing her daughter.

"Lauren?" She glanced up at Grady. "Agent Braun and his tech guys are here."

"Good." She was about to stand up, but Grady placed a hand on her shoulder to keep her seated. No doubt he was still worried about her feet. Wearing the thick fluffy socks had helped ease the soreness.

"He needs to access your phone." Grady gently pried the device from her fingers. "You'll get it back very soon."

"Okay." Logically, she knew that tracing Simon Cromwell's call was important. But she didn't like giving up the only connection to her daughter, even for a few minutes. The tech guys and Agent Braun huddled around the dining room table to discuss the best way to proceed.

She belatedly realized they had likely missed dinner. Her stomach was a knot of tension, but she forced herself to consider the guests in her home. "I can see if there's something to eat in the fridge."

"Don't bother. We're fine." Grady dropped down on the sofa beside her. He took her hands in his. "We're going to find her."

Tears pricked her eyes. "I hope so."

He held her gaze for a moment, then glanced up as the blond-haired man approached. To her surprise, Micah held a handgun toward Grady, butt first. "To replace the one you had to hand over to the cops."

"Thanks." Grady released her hands so he could accept the gun. He turned away and worked the chamber. Then he holstered it and turned back to Micah. "We need to start digging into Jerry Cromwell's background. Maybe he has other properties that his kids are using."

Micah nodded. "Rex brought a laptop along. That's a good place to start."

"What if Jerry Cromwell is out of prison?" She abruptly jumped to her feet. "When we talked about him before, I hadn't paid much attention to him because he was so much older than the guy who took Ariel. But now that we know he has twin sons, it could be that Jerry is out there too."

"I'm on it," Rex said, his fingers flying across the laptop keyboard. "Looks like Jerry Cromwell was released two weeks ago."

"How is that possible?" Her voice was barely a whisper.

"According to this, Jerry Cromwell was diagnosed with end-stage lung cancer." Rex grimaced, glancing between Grady and Micah. "Looks like he was given a compassionate release because he only has six months to live." When she frowned, Rex added, "This is a new thing the prison system is doing. They don't want to provide the care and treatment of these prisoners, and there's always the issue of over-crowding, so they release them so they can be cared for elsewhere."

"We should have thought of digging into Jerry Cromwell earlier," Grady said harshly. She could tell by the way he eyed Agent Braun that he was thinking the FBI should have been on that angle too. But all the self-incriminations in the world wasn't going to change the facts.

They needed to find Lucy!

When a phone rang, there was an abrupt silence. Then it rang again.

"Lauren? It's your phone, someone is calling from an unknown number." Agent Braun's voice was tense. "You need to answer it and keep the kidnapper talking for as long as possible."

She jumped to her feet and crossed to the table. Leaning forward, she hit the button to answer the call. Then she quickly put the call on speaker. "Hello?"

"If you want to see your daughter again, do exactly as I say." She hadn't expected the mechanical voice.

"I will. But I want to hear from Lucy. I need to know she's alive and unharmed."

There was a brief pause, then her daughter's voice said, "Mommy?"

She sagged into the closest empty chair. "I'm here, Lucy. Grady too. You're going to be fine, okay? I love you."

"I love you too."

"Twenty-five million dollars. One million for every year." The mechanical voice was back. "You'll receive instructions within the hour."

"Wait, that's impossible. It's a Friday night! The banks are closed . . ." She stopped, realizing the line was dead.

Simon Cromwell had disconnected after making his outrageous demand.

15

—————

Grady had listened to Lucy's shaky voice on the other end of the ransom call, his gut twisting with fear for the little girl. The anguish etched on Lauren's features didn't help. He hated knowing how much she was suffering. Lucy too.

He turned toward Agent Braun. "Did you get the trace?"

The fed grimaced and gestured to the tech who shrugged. "The call pinged off a tower here." The tech guy tapped the computer screen. Grady leaned in to see better. The area in question was slightly south but mostly west of the Chicago Cultural Center. "There's about a mile radius around the location of the call. Doesn't narrow it down much, I'm afraid."

Simon could have Lucy anywhere within a mile of the dot on the map. With so many people living in the city, Grady needed more, a way of narrowing down the most likely hiding spot. Yet he had no idea of knowing whether they were in a motel or a private residence.

Battling a wave of frustration, he pulled his phone and

called Griff again. The FBI agent out of Wyoming answered on the first ring. "I was just going to call you. Dom found the car at two different locations. The first was at the intersection of Wacker and Monroe; the second sighting was at West Taylor and Morgan Street. Do you know where they are?"

As Griff spoke, he wrenched the computer from the tech guy and zeroed in on the map to identify the most recent sighting. It was only a mile from the pinpointed cell tower. "Yeah, I have the map up for that location now. Looks like there could be a lot of residential homes in that area."

"That's what Dom said," Griff agreed. "I don't know if this helps much, but we wanted you to know."

Rex was working on his laptop, so Grady stepped back, allowing the tech guy access to the screen. "Every little bit helps. Can you ask Dom to search for any property associated with Jerry, Simon, or Shane Cromwell?"

Griff repeated the request for Dom. Then added, "We're on it. What are the Chicago feds doing?"

"They're here." He didn't bother to mention he wasn't impressed with Braun's work on the case so far. The guy had an entire office of agents to help him, and Griff was giving him results faster. "Please keep me updated if you find anything."

"Who was that?" Braun asked with a frown.

"Griff Flannery." Grady held the agent's gaze. "His tech guy was able to find the black SUV at two intersections."

Braun's face flushed, but he simply nodded. "That helps."

You think? It took all of Grady's willpower not to snap. "I want the local police to go knock on the doors of every motel and hotel within a mile of the pinpointed location of the call."

To his credit, Braun didn't argue but reached for his phone to do as Grady demanded.

"We need to search property records too," the tech guy said. "We can find out if any are rentals."

"That's a good idea." Grady liked the fact that each tech expert was working a different angle. Dom was looking for links to the Cromwell name, but searching for rentals in the area was a good plan too.

He glanced at Lauren, who had covered her face in her hands. His heart ached for her, and he wished he'd insisted they stay home from the stupid charity event.

"I think I found something," Rex said, breaking into his thoughts. Grady spun from the table to join his boss. He bent to look over Rex's shoulder to see his laptop screen. "There's a small rental property near the location of the cell tower signal. Looks to be a small house nestled between apartment buildings. It has a red-brick exterior with black shutters."

"What's the address?" Grady asked, his heart thumping with anticipation.

"The address is 910 South Miller Street. It's a few blocks from the last place the car was seen," Rex added.

Grady turned toward the tech analyst. "Any chance we can figure out who rented it?"

"I'm not sure." The lack of confidence was not inspiring.

Grady couldn't stand the idea of sitting there a moment longer. He stood and reached for his coat.

"Where are you going?" Braun demanded.

"I'm going to check the area for myself." He pulled his rental car key fob from his pocket. "I'll call you if I see anything suspicious."

"I'm coming with you." Lauren jumped up from her seat at the table. "I'll get my shoes."

"You can't," Braun protested. "You need to be here to answer your phone when the kidnapper calls again."

"It's not like you were able to trace the call. Besides, I'll call my father on the way." Lauren stared at Grady, her gaze pleading with him. "He may be able to access money from an overseas account to make the ransom."

"Are you sure about this?" He didn't blame Lauren for wanting to ride along. Sitting and doing nothing was painful. But having her there meant he needed to be extra careful. When she nodded and shoved her injured feet into a pair of running shoes and pulled on her leather coat, he sighed. "Let's go."

"You can't just leave . . ." Braun's voice trailed off as they left the apartment, letting the door close softly behind them.

Lauren was silent as they rode the elevator down to the parking garage. He didn't know what to say to make her feel better. He unlocked the car, then opened the passenger door for her. Once they were out on the road, he finally said, "You know the area the best. What's the quickest way to get to the west side of Chicago?"

"Take a right at the next intersection." Lauren's voice was tight but calm. "I need to believe we're going to find her."

"We will." He frowned. "Are you really going to call your father?"

"Yes." She pulled out the new phone and made the call. Her father must have answered, because she said, "Dad? Lucy's been kidnapped, and I need twenty-five million dollars."

Grady focused on driving, mentally reviewing the map he'd looked at earlier in his mind. That Lauren could casually discuss handing over such an astronomical amount of money to a kidnapper was difficult to comprehend. He understood money was nothing compared to a child's life, but he silently vowed there was no way he was letting the Cromwells get away with this.

Kidnapping a wealthy woman's child because you feel as if you were owed something was unacceptable.

"I understand, Dad. I appreciate your efforts." There was a pause, then Lauren added, "I will call you as soon as I hear from them. Thanks."

"What did your dad say?" He couldn't imagine getting money, even from overseas, was possible on a weekend.

"Turn right at the next intersection, then keep heading west." She sighed and shook her head. "It's not good. Dad has some cryptocurrency that we can use, but the banks overseas are closed for the weekend too. I don't know what they're thinking. Being rich doesn't necessarily mean we can get that kind of money day or night." There was a hint of bitterness in her tone.

"That's okay. We're going to find Lucy very soon." His phone rang. Recognizing Griff's number, he handed it to Lauren. "This is Griff. Put the call on speaker, okay?"

She nodded and answered. "Griff, this is Lauren. We're in the car. I'm putting you on speaker so Grady can hear." She did so, then added, "Do you have something?"

"None of the properties in the area are owned by Cromwell," Griff said, getting straight to the point. "We found a rental property in the area, though. We're working on that as a possible location now."

"Is 910 South Miller Street?" Grady asked. "We're heading there now."

"Yeah, it is. You think that's the place?" Griff sounded excited now. "Hang on, Dom is doing his hacker thing to find out more."

Grady glanced at Lauren. Her blue eyes were full of hope. "Please ask Dom to hurry," she said. "They demanded a twenty-five-million-dollar ransom after hours on a Friday night. I don't know what they're going to do if I can't make that happen."

"Lauren, this is Dominic. I can help you do an electronic transfer if you'd like. The good news is that the funds won't be available until Monday morning, so we'd have the weekend to continue working the case."

"Thanks, Dominic." Lauren's voice was strained. "I will gladly pay that to get Lucy back. But I'm worried they'll keep her until they know they can access the funds."

Grady was inclined to agree with Lauren's assessment. They needed to find Lucy before the one-hour deadline. "Let's just see if we can identify where they're holding Lucy."

"I'm on it." Grady heard Dom typing on the computer. "Okay, the good news is that they're using a popular home-sharing app. They've tightened their security, but I think there's a way . . ." Dominic's voice trailed off. Then he said, "I'm in! Give me a minute to look at that specific address."

"We're going to find her," Lauren whispered. "I can feel it."

"Okay, I found that rental property, but it's not being paid for by anyone with the name of Cromwell," Dom said. "The payment was made by a woman by the name of Karla Dalton."

"That's Nelson's girlfriend!" Lauren exclaimed. "She's involved!"

Grady pushed his speed as fast as he dared. He wanted to get to the rental property as quickly as possible. "That's perfect, Dom. You've been a huge help. Thanks. We need to call the police to let them know."

"You do that. Let me know when you have the little girl back." With that, Dom ended the call.

"Call Lieutenant Olson," he said. "Tell him to have

squads meet us at the rental property, but no lights and sirens. We need to approach with caution."

"Okay." Lauren looked both relieved and terrified as she made the call. "Lieutenant Olson?" Grady listened as she repeated his instructions. "Yes, the FBI is at my place, but we don't have time to wait for them to show. You should already have squads in the area, don't you? Okay, thanks." She lowered the phone. "They'll be there in five to ten minutes."

He nodded, slowing to make the turn onto Miller street. "Good. Look for building number 910."

"I think that's it." Lauren leaned forward in her seat. "Third on the west side of the street."

It was indeed a red-brick house with black shutters that was sandwiched between two multifamily units. There was no black SUV parked on the street, but he saw there was a single-car garage door that was closed. The vehicle was likely inside. He drove slowly past the house that had lights shining through the curtained windows.

The setup did not work to their advantage. There was barely a two-foot gap between the rental house and the buildings on either side. He racked his brain for a way to get inside as he drove around the block.

"What's the plan?" Lauren asked, when he pulled over to park several doors down from the rental. There was no street parking allowed, so he kept the vehicle idling. "Are we going to wait for the police to arrive?"

He blew out a breath and turned to look at her. "I'm going to check the place out. You stay here." When she opened her mouth to argue, he held up his hand. "I need you to watch for the police, and I won't be long. I just want to know what we're dealing with."

"Okay." Her expression was one of resolve. "I hope you can see Lucy."

"Me too." He slid out from behind the wheel and jogged across the street. Waiting for the police was the smart way to go, but he was concerned about what Simon and Jerry Cromwell might do.

Jerry, in particular, had nothing to lose. The guy was dying. And Grady had already killed his son Shane. Simon must have known his brother was either dead or arrested.

Either way, Grady couldn't ignore the deep sense of foreboding as he cautiously approached the rental house.

Silently, he prayed for God to grant him the strength and wisdom he needed to rescue Lucy.

LAUREN SAT for a full five minutes before she pushed out of the car. There was no sign of the police yet, so she followed Grady's footsteps and ran across the road. The red-brick rental house was cute enough. Sandwiched between the apartment buildings, she could see why the owners rented the place out.

There was no question in her mind that Nelson was involved in this. He'd likely convinced his girlfriend, Karla, to cooperate to get the money. Then once he was released from prison, they could go anywhere in the world to be together.

When she got closer to the narrow gap between the buildings, her eyes widened in shock when she realized Grady was scaling the house with one hand on each side of the narrow gap, along with both feet also propped on either sider. With his hands and feet braced on each building, he was painstakingly making his way up to the second-story window. The one with a light glowing from inside.

She held her breath as Grady used his incredible

strength to move each foot, then each hand to get higher. When he reached the window, he leaned over to look inside. Then he lightly tapped on the window, drawing someone's attention.

Lucy? Had he found her daughter?

Lauren risked a glance toward the street. Still no police response. Turning her attention back to Grady and the second-story window, her eyes widened when she realized the window was opening.

Then Lucy's head poked out.

Lauren swallowed a gasp, watching as Grady spoke softly to Lucy.

She moved closer. "Grady? I'm here. Hand Lucy down to me."

He looked down at her, then nodded. "Move back, Lucy. I'm coming in."

He was? She wanted to protest as Lucy's head disappeared. In a swift movement, Grady propped himself up by his legs only until he could grab the windowsill with both hands. He pulled himself up and then climbed inside.

She breathed a sigh of relief when she realized he was safe. Then he leaned out to look down at her. "Ready?"

"Yes." She lifted her arms as high as she could.

Grady helped Lucy out of the window, holding her daughter firmly as he gently lowered her out.

"I'm scared," Lucy whimpered.

"I know, but I'm here and so is your mom. We won't let you fall." Grady's voice was reassuring. Lauren braced herself for the impact. Getting Lucy out of there before the police arrived would be amazing. If the little girl didn't fall and break her legs. "Easy now," Grady murmured, holding Lucy beneath her arms and lowering her down.

Lauren could feel Lucy's shoes touch the palms of her

hands. Lauren's cheerleading days were a long time ago, so she didn't have the strength or agility as when she was in high school. Then Grady lowered Lucy a little more, leaning so far out the window now that she feared he'd fall. Lauren wrapped her arms around Lucy's thighs, holding tight.

"Can you brace your hands on the wall?" Lauren whispered.

"Yes." Lucy's voice was strained.

"Grady, let her go." When he did, her muscles bunched with the effort of holding Lucy. But the little girl leaned against the wall, easing the strain. Lauren slowly lowered herself to the ground until Lucy's feet touched the earth.

They'd done it! Lucy was safe! She glanced up at the window, expecting Grady to be climbing out to join them.

But he wasn't there.

"Come, Lucy!" Lauren took her daughter's hand and led her out to the street where she'd left the rental. A police car rolled silently down the street toward them. She lifted her arm to wave, then continued taking Lucy to the vehicle. "Get in the back." She opened the rear passenger-side door. "The police are going to help arrest the men who took you."

"Stay with me," Lucy begged.

She hesitated, glancing back at the house. Grady was inside with at least two kidnappers, maybe three if Karla was in there too. The police cruiser pulled in behind them. "Lucy, I need to warn the police that Grady is in there. Then I'll be back, okay?"

Lucy nodded, shivering. The little girl had been taken from the ballroom and didn't have a coat. She closed the door and hurried over to the police officers who were getting out of the car.

"I'm Lauren Chandler. My daughter Lucy was kidnapped by the men inside that home." She gestured to the red-brick house. "Grady McFarland was able to crawl inside to rescue Lucy. She's safe now. But he's still inside. And I'm sure the kidnappers are armed."

"Get into the car. We'll take over from here," the officer said.

"Okay, but don't shoot Grady. He's not one of the kidnappers." She was afraid the cops would go in with guns blazing.

A second squad arrived with two more officers. The four of them talked for a moment before splitting into two teams to approach the house.

Lauren had crawled in beside Lucy when she heard the sound of gunfire. Her heart lodged in her throat as the officers quickly breached the house.

Lord Jesus, please keep Grady safe in Your care!

Lauren hugged Lucy close as the seconds stretched into minutes. The not knowing was agonizing. Then finally the cops emerged with a younger man and a woman in handcuffs.

Grady? Was he . . .

Then she saw him coming out of the house. Without taking time to think it through, she pushed open her door and ran across the street toward him. She threw herself into his arms, and Grady gathered her close, pressing a kiss to her temple.

"It's over," he whispered near her ear. "Jerry Cromwell is dead."

"Did you . . ." She didn't finish. Really, it didn't matter if he'd been forced to kill the man who'd abducted her twenty-five years ago.

"No, I managed to snag Simon when he came into the room looking for Lucy." Grady leaned back to look into her eyes. "I disarmed him and marched him downstairs. Karla gave in quickly; she wasn't armed. Jerry shot himself rather than risk going back to prison."

"Thank you, Grady. For everything." She wrapped her arms around his neck and drew him in for a kiss.

He kissed her back, and she wished again that it was for real. That Grady cared about her as much as she cared for him.

Not cared, she quickly amended. *Loved*. She'd fallen in love with her fake fiancé/bodyguard.

Yet the nicest thing she could do for him was let him go.

She ended the kiss and pulled away. "I, um, need to get back to Lucy. She's scared out of her mind and doesn't have a coat." Realizing she was babbling, she forced herself to stop and take a breath. She looked Grady squarely in the eye. "Thank you for saving my daughter."

"It's the least I could do." His expression was solemn. "I'm going to make sure Rex reimburses you for my fee. I didn't do my job as well as I had hoped."

"There's no need." Her heart sank as she realized she was just a job to him. "Lucy's kidnapping was my fault, not yours. You risked your life for her more than once. I appreciate everything you've done for me. For us."

"Ms. Chandler?" Lieutenant Olson's voice had her glancing over. "What happened?"

Grady stepped forward. "I found Lucy, climbed in to rescue her, and managed to grab Simon, disarming him." As he went on to describe how the events in the house unfolded, she glanced over to where Lucy was sitting in the car, her face pressed against the window.

Leaving Grady wasn't easy, but she forced herself to cross the street to join Lucy. Grady had his own life, despite how hers now seemed glaringly empty.

To her surprise, Grady came over a few minutes later. He opened the back door, and asked, "Are you ready to go?"

"Yes, please," Lucy said. "I'm cold."

"Take my coat," Grady instantly shrugged out of his jacket and handed it back. "It won't take us long to get back to the apartment."

She wrapped the coat around Lucy's small frame and decided to stay in the back with her daughter. When Grady slid in behind the wheel and pulled away from the curb, she caught his gaze in the rearview mirror. "Did Lieutenant Olson let Agent Braun know that we have Lucy?"

"He was making the call as I left." Grady lifted a shoulder. "You ask me, the cops did more on this case than he did."

She privately agreed. The one loose thread in all this was Nelson. She glanced at Grady, wondering if Karla had mentioned her ex during the arrest. If there was evidence that Nelson had participated in the kidnapping, she prayed his release from prison would be delayed.

Permanently.

By the time they were back in the penthouse, Rex and Micah were the only ones there. Agent Braun and his tech guys had apparently left the moment the danger was over.

"Do you need anything else before we go?" Rex asked.

"No thank you." She wanted to ask Grady to stay but couldn't find the words. "Excuse me for a moment, I need to get Lucy taken care of."

"Of course." Rex nodded.

"Say good night to Mr. Grady," she told her daughter.

"Good night, Mr. Grady." Lucy ran over to give Grady a hug. "Thanks for rescuing me."

"Of course. Good night, Lucy. Sleep well."

Tears pricked her eyes. She blinked them back as she hustled Lucy down the hall to her room.

"They gave me pizza to eat," Lucy said as she changed into her pajamas. "But it wasn't as good as Captain Jack's."

"Well, I'm glad you weren't hurt, sweetie." She hugged Lucy close for a long minute, then leaned back and smoothed the brown hair from her daughter's face. "The danger is over now for good, okay? The bad guys were arrested. You don't have to be afraid any longer."

"Okay." Lucy went into the bathroom, brushed her teeth, and washed her face, then crawled into bed. "Stay with me for a while?"

"Of course." She turned off the lights and stretched out beside Lucy. As she waited for the little girl to fall asleep, she imagined that Rex, Micah, and Grady had likely headed out. She tried not to be upset at not having a chance to tell Grady goodbye.

Maybe it was better this way. She was pretty sure she'd have made a fool out of herself by asking him to stay the weekend.

Fifteen minutes later, she knew Lucy had fallen asleep. Rolling carefully off the bed, Lauren tiptoed across the room and into the hallway. She closed the door, leaving it open just an inch so she could hear if Lucy suffered a nightmare.

She wasn't exactly hungry but decided to grab a yogurt to tide her over until morning. When she stepped into the living room, she stopped abruptly when she saw Grady sitting there.

"Oh, I thought you left." She flushed, then added, "I'm glad you stayed, though. Um, are you hungry? We didn't get to eat our rubbery chicken dinner."

"I could eat." Grady stood and moved toward her. "How's Lucy?"

"She's good." She led the way into the kitchen, hoping Clara had left something edible in the fridge. She opened the door, stared blindly inside for a long moment, then turned to face him. "You were amazing, Grady. Climbing between those buildings like Spiderman? I couldn't believe you were able to get up to save Lucy."

He offered a crooked grin. "I surprised myself. I would have been faster, but my hip was killing me from getting hit by the car."

"What can I get you? Ibuprofen?"

"Nah, I'm fine." He cleared his throat and stepped closer. "Lauren, I know I don't have anything to offer you, but I'd like to see you again. Lucy too," he hastily added. "I don't live in Chicago, but I can stick around for a while . . ."

"Yes. Oh, Grady, yes!" She walked into his arms and drew him down for a kiss. "Yes, I'd love to see you again and again."

"Wow." His low, husky voice sent shivers of awareness down her spine. "You realize I have nothing to offer."

"You have your heart, Grady. And that's more than enough." She stared up at him for a long moment. "I love you. I know it's too soon, but I don't care. I dated Nelson for months, and look how that turned out? I knew the moment we kissed that you were the only man for me."

A slow grin spread across his features. "Good to know, because I've fallen in love with you. Despite your wealth."

"Despite it?" She tipped her head to the side. "Really?"

"Yeah, really. I was prepared to hate you on sight, but you proved yourself to be more than a pampered rich woman." His gaze turned serious. "You're beautiful, Lauren. Inside and out."

"Oh, Grady." She pulled him in for another kiss. "I think that's the nicest thing any man has ever said to me."

"You are," he insisted. "I love you. We'll find a way to make it work." Before she could ask what that meant, he captured her mouth with his.

As she kissed Grady, she realized that this was all that mattered. Love was all they truly needed.

The rest would work out one way or another, according to God's plan.

EPILOGUE

F*our weeks later . . .*
Grady unlocked the front door to his house in Cody, Wyoming, and stepped back so Lauren and Lucy could enter. He wasn't ashamed of his humble abode, although it was a far cry from Lauren's penthouse apartment.

"Grady, this is amazing," Lauren gushed as she stood in the center of the open-concept living room and kitchen. "Look, Lucy, we can see the mountains from here."

"They're so big!" Lucy ran over to the back patio doors to see better. Then she turned back to Grady. "Do wild animals really live there?"

"Yep. Deer, elk, moose, and bears." When Lucy's blue eyes widened, he hastily added, "The bears are still hibernating yet. They don't venture out until April, when the weather gets warmer."

"Wow." Lucy turned back to stare at the mountains. "I wish it was warmer now so I could see the mountains up close."

"We can do a little hiking, if your mom wants to." He

eyed Lauren warily. "If not, that's okay. It was just a suggestion."

"I would love to go hiking, but maybe when the weather warms up." She smiled at him. "It's so peaceful around here without all the traffic noise."

"Yeah, we don't have traffic jams." He couldn't help but smile as Lauren gazed around his house with appreciation. "It's nice and quiet until the summer tourist season."

"I can see why you live here." Lauren glanced at Lucy, then stepped closer. "And you should know I'd never ask you to leave."

He had a plan he wanted to discuss, but he wasn't sure if this was the right time. The danger was over, Simon Cromwell was sitting in jail, and Karla had agreed to testify against Nelson for a lighter sentence for her part in the kidnapping-for-ransom scheme. Nelson had used the prison computers to find the Cromwell twins and had asked Karla to get in touch with them on his behalf. Nelson's release had been revoked in light of the new charges he faced as a result of Lucy's kidnapping.

Lauren had been appalled that Nelson had used her childhood tragedy against her. Grady was just glad the guy would spend even more time behind bars.

"I, uh, have an idea," he managed.

"Can I see the bedrooms?" Lucy asked, interrupting them.

"Sure, go ahead." He didn't look away from Lauren. They'd been seeing each other for the past four weeks, spending most of their time in Chicago. Grady had gotten somewhat used to the penthouse apartment, but he'd wanted Lauren to see his home before he made their fake engagement real. When Lucy disappeared down the hall, he didn't waste a second. "I love you, Lauren." He dipped his hand into his pocket and pulled out a small ring box. "Will you please marry me?"

"Oh, Grady. Yes! I'd love to marry you." She held out her hand so he could slide the diamond engagement ring onto her finger. "The ring is beautiful, thank you."

He knew she could afford something bigger, but he'd come to appreciate how down-to-earth Lauren was, despite her wealth. She didn't make him feel bad for not having as much money, even though he did fairly well working for Rex Grayson.

Well enough that he didn't have to work as many cases now if he chose not to. He kissed her for a long moment, then leaned back to look down at her. "I know this place isn't as fancy as your penthouse, but I was thinking we could split our time between Chicago and Cody. While keeping Lucy's school schedule in mind," he quickly added. "I think she could benefit from spending some time here."

"I completely agree." He was surprised when Lauren didn't argue. "In fact, I think we should make this home here in Cody our primary residence. That way Lucy can go to school here. It hasn't been the same since Ariel's mother moved her daughter to a different school. The only reason to go back to Chicago would be to attend specific charity events." She searched his gaze for a moment. "I'll prioritize those that are most important to me."

"Really?" He hadn't expected this. "Are you sure? Maybe you should see what it's like here in the dead of winter."

She arched a brow. "Winters are long and cold in Chicago too. Besides, I'm looking forward to a more laid-back lifestyle." She smiled. "I love you, Grady. This town, this rural setting is part of you. And I like it too."

Maybe she was just saying that to make him feel better, but he wasn't going to complain. They had time to figure things out. "I love you, very much." He kissed her again, thinking he was the luckiest man on earth. Then Lucy skipped down the hall, interrupting them.

"Hey, did you ask Mom to marry you yet?" Lucy demanded. "You're not supposed to kiss her unless you're going to get married."

"I did ask her, and she said yes." He grinned at Lauren's surprised expression. "Lucy made me wait until we were here in Wyoming to ask you."

"Yay!" Lucy jumped up and down with joy. "I get to have Grady as a dad!"

Lauren laughed and drew Lucy in for a three-way hug. Grady thought his heart would burst from being so full of love.

Love for God, for Lauren, and for his new family.

I hope you enjoyed *Deadly Abduction*, the first book in my new series. Are you ready for Micah and Bryn's story in *Deadly Reunion*? Click here!

DEAR READER

Thanks for reading *Deadly Abduction*! I hope you enjoyed Grady and Lauren's story. It's exciting to start a new series, and I hope you continue reading the next books in my Grayson's Guardians series. The next book will be Micah's story in *Deadly Reunion*.

Don't forget, you can purchase ebooks or audiobooks directly from my website and will receive a 15% discount by using the code **LauraScott15.**

I adore hearing from my readers! I can be found through my website at https://www.laurascottbooks.com, via Facebook at https://www.facebook.com/LauraScottBooks, Instagram at https://www.instagram.com/laurascottbooks/, and Twitter https://twitter.com/laurascottbooks. Please take a moment to subscribe to my YouTube channel at youtube.com/@LauraScottBooks-wr1xl?sub_confirmation=1. Also take a moment to sign up for my monthly newsletter to learn about my new book releases! All subscribers receive a free novella not available for purchase on any platform.

Until next time,

Laura Scott

PS: Keep reading for a sneak peek of *Deadly Reunion* . . .

DEADLY REUNION

Chapter One

Bryn Sinclair unlocked the back door to her house and stepped across the threshold, exhaustion from the long day of dealing with law enforcement over her missing boss weighing heavily on her shoulders. She frowned when she caught a whiff of a strange scent.

Someone was inside!

She froze, straining to listen. With her heart thudding painfully against her sternum, she took a silent step back. The door had been locked, so she wasn't sure how the intruder had gotten in. Holding her breath, she took another step back, hoping and praying whoever was inside didn't know she'd come home.

A crack of gunfire split the night air.

Bryn whirled and ran, ducking her head to make herself a smaller target. Her purse thudded against her side. She gathered it close and continued to run. More gunfire rang out, but she didn't slow her pace. Fearing she'd be shot at any second, she ran with all the strength she could muster, heading toward the wooded area behind her house. Her car was in the detached garage, and she didn't think there was time to use her vehicle to escape. Instead, she hoped the gunman wouldn't be familiar with the area the way she was.

After everything that had happened earlier that day, she numbly realized she should have anticipated this.

But she hadn't. And now that lapse in judgment might get her killed.

With a frantic burst of speed, she reached the wooded section of Chicory Park. Due to the April time change, it was still too light for her peace of mind. Dusk had fallen, but she was afraid the gunmen would be able to see her red quilted jacket through the trees.

Who was shooting at her? This had to be related to Damien Rochester's disappearance. Her life was normally boring. Routine. As exciting as sliced bread.

Until today when the police had come looking for her absent boss.

Bryn made her way deeper into the park preserve, avoiding the marshlands. She didn't hear anything that indicated the gunman had followed her. She stopped beside a tree, leaning weakly against the trunk as she caught her breath. She lived in a small residential area north of Madison, Wisconsin. She'd moved there from St. Louis when she'd gotten the job offer to work for Damien Rochester as his personal assistant.

Now, she wished she'd have stayed in Missouri.

What was left of the evening light faded away, cloaking her in darkness. Grateful for the coverage, she pushed away from the tree and made her way through to the opposite side of the park. Bryn stepped carefully, feeling the spongy marshland give beneath her feet, her low-heeled flats getting damp from the water. She sought higher ground. The last thing she wanted was to be stuck out there. She knew the Yahara River snaked through the park toward Lake Mendota. Madison was not only the Wisconsin state capital, but it was flanked by two large lakes, making it a great place to live and work.

If your boss wasn't Damien Rochester, she thought darkly. Where was he anyway? She couldn't imagine he was the one who'd been in her house, shooting at her. It wasn't as if he'd have a reason to silence her.

Her left foot sank into the muck. With a grimace, she yanked free and changed her course. Again. After what seemed like an eon, she caught a glimpse of light. Winding through the trees, she used the light as a beacon. When she broke free of the woods, she breathed a sigh of relief when she saw the sign was for O'Brien's Pub.

"Thank you, Lord," she whispered, quickening her pace to reach the building. Bryn needed help, fast. And not just from her Divine Savior.

Her friends were all coworkers. Calling Gwen, Sam, Tabitha, or one of the others wasn't an option. Not after everything that had gone down earlier today. No, there was only one person here on earth she could trust. Micah Newton, her older brother's best friend.

Tommy was gone, killed during the army troops' withdrawal from Afghanistan. She hadn't seen Micah since Tommy's funeral five years ago.

Yet she knew that if she called, Micah would answer. Out of a sense of duty toward her brother, if nothing else.

Bryn swiftly walked into the pub, taking a moment to look around before heading toward an empty table in the corner. By some miracle, she hadn't lost her purse, so she quickly rummaged inside for her phone. Ignoring her trembling fingers, she scrolled through her contact list until she found Micah. A server approached with a menu.

"Thanks." Bryn took the menu. "I'll need a little time before I order." Bryn wasn't sure staying in the pub was smart. If the gunman was still out there looking for her, this place might be too obvious. What if he walked in through the front door? The thought made her shiver.

"Would you like anything to drink?" the server asked.

"Not yet." Bryn pressed Micah's name on the screen and held the phone to her ear. The pub was loud, so she stuck her finger in her other ear to hear better. Micah, bless him, answered on the first ring.

"Bryn? Are you okay?" Micah's voice held concern, no doubt because she hadn't called him despite his offer to get together after Tommy's funeral.

"Not really. I—something's going on. My boss disappeared, and the police questioned me at length. Then there was someone waiting for me at my house when I got home. He fired shots at me, so I ran."

"Fired shots?" Micah's voice rose in alarm. "Where are you now?"

"At O'Brien's Pub north of Madison." She swallowed hard. "Micah? I'm scared. The pub isn't far from my place. What if the gunman comes after me?"

"Call the police." Micah's voice was firm. "Let them know what happened. I'll make my way to Madison, but I'm in Chicago. It's going to take a while."

Her heart sank. Chicago was a good two-hour drive or more from where she was. Yet she belatedly realized she should have thought of calling the police. That's what a normal person would do.

The problem was that she'd just spent hours being grilled by the police who seemed to think she knew more than she did about Damien's disappearance. By the time she was two hours into the interview, she'd realized the police considered her a suspect. They believed she knew exactly where Damien was hiding. Her denial fell on deaf ears.

Tears pricked her eyes. Would calling the police about the shooting at her home help her case or make her situation worse? Bryn wasn't sure. Either way, staying put wasn't an option. Sliding off the barstool, she hurried back outside. She turned away from the parking lot and walked toward the side of the building that was farthest from the road.

"Micah, there's something going on. I can't explain now, it's too complicated, but I don't want to call the police. I need to get out of here, but my car is back at my house."

"Don't go home." Micah's blunt statement sounded like an order. "Can you get to the airport in Madison? I can arrange for a rental car to be waiting there for you."

Glancing around, she tried to ignore the feeling she was being watched. She went around to the back of the building, wrinkling her nose at the awful stench from the dumpster. Was the gunman still out there? Or was she just being paranoid? Gathering her scattered thoughts, she forced herself to answer. "Yes. I can get a rideshare to the airport."

There was a brief pause. "Is it too far for you to walk?"

"I ran into Chicory Park and headed in the opposite direction from the airport." She had no idea how far she'd gone. "I'm wearing stupid shoes, which makes it difficult to walk long distances. Besides, I feel exposed out here."

"Okay, then take a rideshare," Micah said. "I'll make sure the car is waiting. I want you to head south toward me. We'll meet someplace halfway, okay?"

"I understand." She hunched her shoulders against the cold. Her feet were wet and sore from running. Her flat-soled office shoes were not meant for hiking. "But, Micah? Please hurry. I'm scared."

"I'll be there as quickly as possible. And don't be scared." His voice gentled. "If you need to talk, call me back."

"Okay. Thanks." She felt slightly better when she lowered the phone and pulled up a rideshare app. She arranged for a ride that was only five minutes away. Watching the progress of the driver approach the pub on her phone screen, she waited until the car appeared to be pulling into the parking lot before leaving the safety of the building.

The rideshare driver was behind the wheel of a silver sedan. Sprinting across the parking lot, she wrenched the back door open and slid inside. "Horacio?" she asked as she eyed the driver, matching his face with the one on her screen.

"Yes, are you Bryn Sinclair?" The Hispanic driver's brown eyes met hers in the rearview mirror. "You're going to the airport?"

"Yes, please. Thanks." She wanted to scream at him to hurry as he slowly turned around in the parking lot and headed back out onto the road.

After clicking her seatbelt into place, she turned to look behind them, half expecting more gunfire.

But there was nothing but silence.

She tried to relax as Horacio drove toward the airport. She'd only been to the airport a handful of times, but that was only to pick up Damien after his trips. She'd always stayed out in the car, never going inside. She had no idea where the rental car counters were located.

Damien. Just thinking of him made her blood boil. If her boss was guilty of embezzling money from the company, she hoped and prayed that he'd be found and arrested very soon.

MICAH NEWTON PUSHED the speed limit as much as he dared as he headed north toward Wisconsin. He didn't want to get pulled over and knew the cops monitored speeders via the tollway, but every nerve in his body screamed at him to reach Bryn as soon as possible.

What was going on? Who had fired shots at her? As much as he wanted answers, his first call was to his boss, Rex Grayson of Grayson's Guardians.

"Yeah?" Rex's voice was wary.

"I've got a problem." Micah got straight to the point. "I'm going to need resources to help Bryn Sinclair out of a jam."

"Tommy's younger sister? That Bryn Sinclair?" Rex sounded concerned. "What happened?"

"I'm not sure why, but someone fired shots at her. She took off running, and when she was safe, she called me for help." Micah moved over to get around a semitruck. "I arranged for a rental car using our corporate account. She's on her way to the Madison airport now."

Micah wasn't too concerned about the money, but he didn't want to hide anything from his boss either. Rex knew Bryn's older brother Tommy had been killed during the exfil that had gone sideways. "That's fine. But who is after her? And why?"

"That's what I intend to find out." Micah hated knowing he was so far away. "I just wanted you to know I'm basically hiring us on her behalf."

"That goes without saying." Rex shrugged that off, the

way Micah knew he would. "We take care of our own. Protecting Bryn is the least we can do."

"Yeah." Micah bit back a curse as taillights flared with a traffic jam up ahead. He smacked his palm against the steering wheel. He did not need a construction delay. "I've asked her to head south so we can meet halfway."

"What do you need from me?" Rex asked. "I can see if the other guys are available to help."

"Don't worry about that now. I'm the closest, right?" When Rex didn't argue, he added, "I'll let you know when I have Bryn."

"Okay, but if you need anything, I'm just a phone call away," Rex said.

"Thanks." Micah ended the call. He knew everyone from the team would gladly help if needed.

Only twelve men and women had survived the horrific exfil that day. Twelve out of thirty. It was a loss that haunted all of them, but as their captain, Rex had taken it harder than most. The twelve who remained were Rex, Grady, Micah, Stone, Regan, Cameron, Nolan, Houston, Dina, Theo, Teagan, and Zander.

Micah mourned the loss of their team too. They shouldn't have been ambushed that day. If things had been done properly, but they hadn't been. And good people had been killed as a result of idiots sitting behind a desk who didn't know what they were doing.

He swallowed hard and thrust the thought aside. He couldn't change the past. All he could do was push forward. Yet there was no denying his guilt was centered on the fact that he'd made it out alive when Bryn's brother Tommy hadn't. He and Tommy had joined the army together. They were best friends. If anyone should have died that day, it should have been him. Not Tommy. Micah didn't have family who would grieve over his passing. His mother had dumped him in foster care after his alcoholic father had died. Last he'd heard, his mother had passed away too. Not that losing either parent had mattered much to him.

Tommy did. He and Tommy had been very close. So much so that Micah had expected Bryn to hate him for being the one to come home. But she'd surprised him. Her faith in God, her acceptance that Tommy was in a better place now, had humbled him.

Even if Micah didn't share her steadfast belief.

Traffic around him moved at a crawl. If he had paid closer attention, he'd have noticed the lane closure ahead. When his phone rang, Bryn's name flashed on the screen. He quickly answered.

"Bryn? Are you okay?"

"I'm in the rental car, yes. Thanks for making the arrangements." Her voice still sounded strained. "I'm currently driving south on Highway 51."

"Good. That's perfect. Do you know the city of Beloit? It's on the Illinois-Wisconsin border. It's not a huge city like Madison, but it's not that small either. Let's meet there." He breathed a sigh of relief that the congested traffic eased up once he made it through the bottleneck. "If I'm late, find a public place like a restaurant."

"Beloit?" Her tone was hesitant. "I've never been there."

"Me either." He tried to sound reassuring. "Don't worry, we'll be together very soon."

"I appreciate your help on this, Micah. Thank you."

"Hey, what are friends for?" He hoped his casual tone didn't sound forced.

She sniffled, and he hoped she wasn't crying. "Thanks. I'll see you soon."

"Bryn, try not to worry. I promise to keep you safe."

"I know. I just hope you don't regret it." Her comment had him frowning in confusion, but then she added, "I'll explain everything once I see you."

He would have preferred to keep her on the line, but he didn't want either of them to drive distracted. Especially as he navigated the construction zone. "I'm looking forward to it. Just relax and keep heading south."

"I will." With that, she ended the call.

Micah frowned at the blank screen on his console but squelched the urge to call her back. She was in a rental car and would soon be out of the city. He wasn't sure what was going on, but he felt good about the fact that she'd called him for help.

This was the least he could do for Tommy's little sister.

As Micah drove, Tommy's last words echoed in his mind. The ambush had caught all of them off guard. When Tommy went down, Micah had spun to return fire, then bent down to hoist his buddy to his feet. Blood oozed from Tommy's belly, and the guy had leaned heavily on him as Micah half dragged, half carried him toward the waiting plane. Rex was standing just inside the plane, grabbing soldiers and pulling them inside between firing rounds over their heads to keep the insurgents at bay.

Then another bullet had struck Tommy, and all of Micah's strength couldn't keep him from falling to the ground. Micah knelt beside Tommy, screaming at his buddy to hang on as he hauled Tommy up and over his shoulder in a fireman's carry.

The sound of gunfire continued to echo around them. Micah still wasn't sure how he'd found the strength and endurance to carry Tommy all the way up the plank and into the plane. He dropped Tommy on the ground, shouting for Doc, a.k.a. Regan Harmon, to help.

Tommy's eyes had fluttered open when Doc put pressure on his bleeding wound. For a moment, his buddy looked confused, but then his gaze had focused on Micah. "Take . . . care of . . . Bryn."

Tommy's eyes had closed, and within minutes, his buddy was gone.

Take care of Bryn. Take care of Bryn. Take care of Bryn.

The plea echoed in his mind like some sort of mantra. But it was worse now because someone had tried to kill Bryn, and he had no idea who or why.

Beloit was still forty-five miles away. Thankfully, he was moving at a faster pace now. Micah hoped he'd reached Beloit at the same time Bryn did. She'd had to backtrack to get to the airport, but from there, the ride down shouldn't take more than an hour.

An hour that would feel like an eternity.

By the time Micah was fifteen minutes out of Beloit, his nerves were stretched thin. He was reaching over to call Bryn when his phone rang. Seeing her name on the screen, he was struck by a wave of relief.

"Bryn? Are you in Beloit?"

"Yes. I'm at the Turtle Creek Grill. It's a restaurant in the center of town." Her voice sounded stronger now. "Do you think you can find it?"

"Absolutely. I'm about fifteen minutes away, maybe less. Go ahead and eat if you're hungry."

"I'll wait for you." The edge was back in her tone. "I'm at a booth in the back corner."

"I'll be there soon." Now that he wasn't on the tollway, Micah stomped his foot down on the accelerator. The urge to reach Bryn's side was strong. He could tell she felt vulnerable after everything that had happened.

"Thanks, Micah." Once again, she ended the connection

before he was ready. Traffic had lightened up the closer he got to the border. He glanced at the signs, hoping to see one for the Turtle Creek Grill.

Thankfully, the restaurant was off the main road going through town. He pulled over and pushed out of the car. Hurrying inside, he swept his gaze over the patrons until he saw Bryn's shoulder-length red hair.

She rose to her feet as he approached. Then suddenly she was in his arms, holding him tightly. He cradled her close, hoping she wasn't crying again.

"Hey, it's okay. I'm here." He patted her back reassuringly. "You're safe now."

"Oh, Micah." Her voice hitched, and she sniffled again, before lifting her head to look up at him. "I think this is partially my fault."

"I doubt that." He tucked a strand of her hair behind her ear. "Let's get something to eat, okay? Then you can tell me all about it."

With a nod, she stepped back and swiped at her eyes. Then she slid back into the booth. Micah didn't take the seat across from her, mostly because he wanted to keep an eye on the front door. Also because he wanted them to be able to speak without anyone overhearing.

They'd barely gotten settled when their server hurried over. She was young and had a purple streak in her hair. "What can I get you to drink?"

"Just water for now." He glanced at Bryn, who had the menu open on the table before her. "We'll order food in a few minutes."

Their server left, returning a moment later with the water. Ignoring the menu, he turned toward Bryn. "What would you like to eat?"

"I'm not hungry." He scowled and arched a brow. She sighed. "Okay, I'll have a club sandwich."

"Great." He gestured for purple streak to come back. "We'll have two club sandwiches with fries."

"Anything else?"

"Nope." He waited for her to leave, then turned to Bryn. "Please start at the beginning."

She nodded and reached for her water. Then she drew in a deep breath. "I work for a public relations and marketing firm by the name of Digital Creative Express. It's co-owned by two men, Richard Freeman and Damien Rochester."

"Go on," he encouraged when she fell silent.

"I'm Damien's personal assistant. I've been with him for the past four years." She stared down at her hands. "I—we were involved briefly, but I ended it a few months ago."

"Involved?" He battled a wave of jealousy. Bryn's personal life was none of his business.

"We dated. I know, it was stupid." She blew out a breath and finally met his gaze. "I don't know what I was thinking. Anyway, Damien didn't seem to mind that I ended it. I thought everything was going fine, then he didn't show up for work yesterday."

He searched her gaze. "And that's unusual?"

"Very. Damien never misses work. I keep his calendar. I knew he didn't have any meetings or trips planned." She dropped her gaze to her hands. "I called his cell phone, but it went to his voice mail. He doesn't have a landline, so I kept trying his cell phone without ever getting an answer."

"Okay." He frowned. "Maybe the guy was just home sick. Everyone gets sick at some point."

"I drove past his condo on my way home. His car wasn't

in the garage, and nobody answered the door." Her voice dropped. "I wasn't sure what to think. Damien and Richard have owned this company for seven years. I didn't tell Richard or his assistant Gwen about Damien being gone. I thought I'd just wait another day."

"Okay, so then what happened?" Micah asked.

"Today, the police showed up at the office around lunchtime. There was still no sign of Damien, and my calls still went to his voice mail."

"Why were the police there? Had someone reported him missing?"

"Yes. Apparently, Richard called them." She met his gaze, tears brimming in her eyes. "Richard accused me of helping Damien embezzle funds from the company. He demanded to know where Damien was hiding out. I tried to tell them I didn't know where he was or anything about missing funds, but nobody believed me. Even Gwen eyed me with suspicion." She used her napkin to wipe her eyes. "The police questioned me for hours. Then when I got home, I smelled something funny and knew someone had been inside my house. I didn't go all the way in. I stepped back just as the gunman fired. He missed me, and that's when I ran."

Micah stared at her in shock. This was far more convoluted than he'd anticipated. "Are you sure Damien didn't take the money?"

"I don't know. If he did, I wasn't involved. I'm innocent, Micah. Of everything except being foolish enough to date my boss." Her eyes filled with tears again. "I'm sorry, but I didn't know who else to call."

"We'll figure this out." Micah injected confidence into his tone, but the truth was, he had no idea how they'd manage that. The first item on the agenda would be to try to find Damien.

But deep down, he feared Damien had purposefully set up Bryn to take the fall for his illegal actions.